scar

scar

Alice Broadway

SCHOLASTIC

For Dave. My love.

Scholastic Children's Books
An imprint of Scholastic Ltd
Euston House, 24 Eversholt Street, London, NW1 1DB, UK
Registered office: Westfield Road, Southam, Warwickshire, CV47 0RA
SCHOLASTIC and associated logos are trademarks and/or
registered trademarks of Scholastic Inc.

First published in the UK by Scholastic Ltd, 2019

Text copyright © Alice Broadway, 2019

The right of Alice Broadway to be identified as the
author of this work has been asserted.

ISBN 978 1407 17286 6

A CIP catalogue record for this book
is available from the British Library.

Printed by CPI Group (UK) Ltd, Croydon, CR0 4YY
Papers used by Scholastic Children's Books are made
from wood grown in sustainable forests.

1 3 5 7 9 10 8 6 4 2

www.scholastic.co.uk

Chapter One

My chin hits gravel; teeth on tongue.

The foot on my back is Jack Minnow's. He presses harder, enjoying the sight of a new believer forced to worship. I spit blood and dust from my lips and Mayor Longsight's bare foot is sprayed red. He leans down and whispers.

"Welcome home, Leora. I have so much to tell you."

I spit again, this time aiming right for him.

The crowd – a respectful distance away from their leader – only see me bow. And they roar their approval – not joy at my return, but jubilation at Mayor Longsight standing above me, above them, ruling over his people. A man, made divinity.

I thought we were safe, I thought everything was new. I thought that Longsight was dead.

Jack Minnow's strong hands drag me to my feet, grasp my hair and hold my head rigid. He turns me to face the townspeople, who hush enough to listen. I stare out at the crowd, at the people I thought were my friends. People I grew up with. My eyes searching for Gull. I can't see her.

"Here is your traitor." Longsight's voice is triumphant. "Here is the one who brought the enemy to our door and an assassin to our square."

A horrible growl rises from the gathered herd of people. The mayor waits for it to ease. "But, friends, what she intended for evil, I have used for good. She planned my destruction, and yet, I wrought my resurrection. There is a higher purpose, and even the wicked plans of a traitor cannot halt true destiny. Do not be worried or afraid. I have conquered."

I shake my head, regretting it immediately when I feel Minnow's fingers tangle in my hair and the ache and sting of my injured mouth. Minnow releases my hair and grasps my arm, pulling me with him towards the dark doors of the government building.

"Time for us to talk," Mayor Longsight says as he follows us inside.

Chapter Two

Mayor Longsight's study is not new to me. But this time, it feels different. The previous times he has always needed me, just a little. He needed me to go to Featherstone; I was the only one who would get away with being his spy. And he needed me again when he wanted to parade me as his puppet. Now I am afraid that he doesn't need me at all.

My stomach turns as the smells of the room swelter around me. Leather and sweat and unread books and polished wood. A metallic top note makes me think of weapons – of sharpened blades – but, when I wet my lips with my swollen tongue, I know it is just the smell of blood. I will get used to that.

I stand there, legs quivering. Jack Minnow's breath is on the back of my shoulder, but he doesn't hold me or attempt to keep me restrained – I pose no threat, not any more. I could try to run, but they would stop me before I reached the door. Besides, I'm tired of running – it never seems to get me anywhere.

There's a feline satisfaction about Mayor Longsight. He has wrapped himself in a burgundy robe and lounges on his chair, one leg crossed over the other, his elbow on the armrest, propping his chin on his hand. His smile is wide and his eyes blink slowly – as though he knows a secret that is hidden from mere mortals. He is alive. It is impossible, unbelievable and yet. . .

"Aren't you going to ask me my secret?" He raises an eyebrow, head cocked to one side as he examines me. "I mean, aren't you just a little bit impressed? It's not every day that someone returns to life."

"I'm impressed by your gall." I'm startled by how cool and steady my own voice sounds. I daren't let him know how shocked I am – that I am finding it next to impossible to process all I am seeing. "I'm impressed that you would play a game like this on such a scale. But then, you do love to trick your people. You weren't resurrected." I summon a sour smile. "The only miracle here is that they believe you."

"And you don't." It's not a question, and his face sinks into thoughtful disappointment. After a while, he stands and steps around the table towards me. I catch glimpses of his beautiful skin as the robe shifts. It seems as though he is almost alight: he gleams darkly, like an ember. I feel that if I touched him my skin would burn. "I'm sorry you doubt me." He stands close – close enough for me to feel the warmth from his body. "But, look—" He shakes off the silken robe and stands with his arms spread wide, so I can see every scrap of ink, every outline of muscle. "You saw the blood. You watched the attack."

I try not to think about it, I tell my memory not to replay that moment, but it's too late and I see him, stabbed and on the ground, pooling blood. I see the cloaked figure of Sana, triumphant. She killed him... Or at least, I thought—

"You remember that morning, I can see it in your face. Look at me, Leora. Look at me now."

The scar is impossible to miss.

A darker line in that tender space just below his ribs, a flash of pink too. Three fingers across. An angry, fierce wound. He should be dead. He was dead.

"How?" My voice is barely a breath. I stretch out a hand.

Longsight laughs, delighted.

Minnow stands close behind me. "You do not touch him," he warns.

"Oh, come now, Jack," Longsight says. "Let her touch – let her examine me. After all, it's the only way she will believe; and you know how much I adore a new convert." He looks at me, challenging me to say no – willing me to say yes.

Before I know what I'm doing, my hand is on his warm

skin. I kneel down to get a closer look, pressing close to the wound and looking up at Longsight to see if he will wince or turn away in pain, but he smiles down at me beatifically as though my interrogation is an act of worship.

It's only a scar, I tell myself. But this – this is the scar of a man who was slain.

Chapter Three

The fragile moment of my fingers on Mayor Longsight's skin is broken when someone raps sharply on the door. Longsight pulls on his robe as though he had simply been showing me some new ink, and Minnow goes to answer, speaking quietly. I stand, rubbing my knees where the carpet has left its plush fuzz on my trousers. The door closes and Minnow, like a dog, attacks, his hand at my throat, pinning me against the bookshelf.

"You brought a blank into Saintstone? How dare you desecrate this town?"

They have found Gull. Hot fear sweeps over me, fear that has nothing to do with Minnow. Gull will never survive the rage of Saintstone.

"Enough, Jack," Longsight says sharply and Jack Minnow stills, chest rising and falling, his hot breath on my face. His hand does not move. The mayor steps close, as though examining the spoils brought by his hunt.

"A blank?" Longsight muses. "Oh, Leora, I thought

you were clever. Bringing a blank here just announces yourself as our enemy."

I try to swallow but my throat is tight and sore against Minnow's hand. I can't speak to reply.

"You have polluted our purity. And you have done your friend no favours. Did you think they would be tolerated here? Still. . ." He looks at me thoughtfully. "She must be kept safe, away from the townspeople. For now. I will speak with her."

Abruptly, Jack Minnow lets me go. I rub my throat. Mayor Longsight had me in his web already but now that he has Gull I am stuck fast. He chuckles and sits back down at his desk, barely concealing his delight as he watches my cheeks burn and my eyes spark with angry tears.

What does he hope to gain from me? What more can he want? He already has the people's devotion – they loved him before, but now that he has cheated death, they adore him. He has all the power and prestige that anyone could ever need and still it isn't enough.

His head is inclined as he considers my fate.

"I have plans for you, Leora Flint. We were counting on your return – expecting you: you always do come back. And now that you're here I can really begin. . . But patience is key. There is no rush." His gaze is thoughtful. I swallow and glance at Minnow – he doesn't speak. Mayor Longsight examines me coolly and eventually sighs. "You will be useful, extremely useful – in time. The question is, what to do with you for now?"

He tips his head at Minnow. "Send a messenger for Mel – tell her to be ready at the lower doors."

Minnow goes out. "I want to see my mother," I announce.

Mayor Longsight laughs.

"Nice try, Leora. Firstly, you don't get to choose. And secondly, your mother won't be coming. Even if we summoned her, she would refuse to see you."

Words, just words, I think. Words designed to hurt and scare me. "I don't believe that," I say calmly while my heart races and my knees shake.

"You're hardly popular in Saintstone, Leora. You are a traitor who brought blanks into our midst."

"She doesn't believe that. She knows me."

"She knows terrible suffering because of you. She is despised and rejected because of you. A pariah in her own town. No wonder, then, that she denounced you. You've brought her nothing but trouble – at least leave her in peace, Leora."

I am silent. Mum would never denounce me. She wouldn't. I know that much.

He smiles gently. "It would be easier if you just accepted that you no longer have a mother. You will stay where I command."

"I'm a prisoner?" I ask, and Longsight raises his eyebrows.

"A prisoner? Oh, that's a bit crass. Let's just stay that you will remain here as my guest. If you care about your blank friend, that is."

My mind swims, as though I am shipwrecked and watching all the things I care about floating further away, sinking to the depths. Minnow returns, and gives Longsight a brief nod.

Longsight gives a languid smile as he stands and smooths down his robe. "Walk with me, Leora."

Minnow holds me tightly, one hand at my shoulder, the other clasping my wrists. I had expected Mayor Longsight's pace to be quick and purposeful, but he walks slowly down the corridors of the government building, nodding graciously to staff who back against the wooden-panelled walls and bow their heads. In contrast to his relaxed presence, Minnow seems bulky and awkward.

"I can't tell you how good it feels to no longer fear death," Longsight purrs as we walk.

"You believe you will live for ever?" I can't keep the scorn from my voice. Longsight merely raises a shoulder as if to say, *just look at me.* "So . . . what did you do? How did you work this supposed miracle? Did you have to say magic words or go through rituals?" I sound dismissive, sarcastic, but really, I'm desperate to know what has happened, how it is that he walks by my side when he should be flayed and made into a skin book.

"Ah, your curiosity has finally been piqued. I knew it wouldn't be long. I'll tell you what happened, gladly – I have no secrets from my people, and I would still like to believe that you are one of us, Leora. But first, a little background." He is quiet for a minute while we walk past people in the passageway and all we hear are their hushed voices and our footsteps. We turn a corner and he resumes.

"It's one thing knowing one's destiny. It's quite another to live it." I think of all the times I have been told that I was born for this moment – that I am a symbol, a sign, a bridge. "I had only ever trusted Jack here with my deepest thoughts and, as good a listener as you are, Jack, I could see that the sceptic within you won every time." He smiles. "I forgive you that, of course. It is not easy to accept change."

He stops to look at a painting that is hung on the wall and Jack shuffles to a halt, pulling me back before I bump into the mayor. The painting shows Saint, our saviour, whose likeness is at the centre of our town. It shows him walking, back turned to the viewer, along a long path. The ground beneath his feet is as red as a carpet welcoming royalty. It is red with the blood that seeps from his body with every step – for, of course, he is walking home to Saintstone, away from the blanks whose wicked leader skinned him as punishment for bringing them his good message of hope. The story I grew up with, the story I heard so often it was embedded in my bones.

I know a different story now.

"It's a great story," Mayor Longsight says as he gazes at the image. "The thing not many people ask, though, is 'What happened next?' What happened after Saint reached Saintstone?"

"Well, that's because we know," I reply. "He arrived back home, wrapped in his skin like a kingly robe, and he was welcomed as a hero. He is the reason our dead are flayed." My voice is dangerously bored. Minnow's fingers squeeze painfully on my wrists. A warning. But Longsight just gives a small smile – humouring me.

"I'm glad you've not forgotten. But that's not what I mean. What happened after *that*?"

I shrug. "Don't tell me – they made him mayor and he was just like you?" Longsight loves to proclaim himself as the new Saint and so, I fling all the hate I have into the word, *mayor*.

Longsight glances at Minnow and nods minutely and Jack twists his grip until the pain is so great that my knees give way.

"Don't test my patience," Longsight says, in a tone that is light and sweet, as though he is talking to a puppy. I get back to my feet, my eyes smarting with pain.

"I imagine he would have been a fine mayor, Leora,"

Longsight carries on. "But he never got the chance. He lived long enough to hear the people's applause and to tell his tale . . . but then he died. We don't tell that bit, because we all prefer a hero to a human." Mayor Longsight sets off walking again. "It's a useful storyteller's device – if you leave someone alive at the end of your story, your listener doesn't have to think about their death. It's in good taste, but it's not the whole truth."

And he's right, I think. *Everyone in the stories lives happily ever after.*

It makes me think of another story: before I knew I had another mum, I never longed for anyone else. It was only when I heard about Miranda and was told the tale of her life and of her death that I missed her, grieved her. Nothing new had happened – it had always been so – but I suddenly felt the heaviness of loss like it might pull me under. Nothing had changed, except my story.

"My story is different," says Longsight. "My story does not end with a death – no, for my death was just a beginning. When the storytellers speak of me, they will never say 'he was' – only 'he is'."

"And you foresaw this?" I ask curiously. "You knew you were . . . *immortal*?"

"I knew there was something special about me, yes," he says. "That I was different – as though my ancestors had set me aside for their own purposes. And the people

13

could feel it too – they said that I was Saint reborn, come for a new era of hope, power and change."

People did speak of him that way, in his election campaign and beyond. I had felt the same. Dan Longsight gave us all a feeling that something better was coming. I loved him for it, once. I wish I could say that even then I saw through him, that my gut instinct had warned me to distrust him, but it would be a lie. I had been as taken in as everyone else. Well, almost everyone else – the crows weren't fooled. Connor, Oscar and Obel, and the other rebels. Dad. Why hadn't he told me?

"You tried to talk me out of it, didn't you, Jack?" Longsight says. Minnow says nothing in response, and Longsight, smiling, carries on. "When I shared my plan with you – to lure Sana, to allow her to commit the act she had been desperate for for so long – I believe it left you shocked." Minnow's eyebrows raise momentarily, and I wonder how shocked he was. Hadn't Sana said she and Jack had worked together? "I saw the doubt in your eyes: why invite your enemy to your quarters? Why make it so easy for them? Why choose death? But now you understand. I reached the high office of mayor because I am deliberate, clever, and because I have very little time for pity."

"And because you're special," I say blandly.

"And because of that." He smiles at me. "We knew that Sana would not be able to resist a public spectacle – we fed information to the crows so that she knew when and where the public address would happen. It was too good for her to resist – a chance to catch us unawares, or so she thought. An opportunity not only to defeat the leader of her enemies, but to do it right in front of them."

I almost – almost – feel sorry for Sana. She was tricked. The only question was how.

"The knife had blood on it when I found it in Featherstone," I say.

"Of course it had blood on it," Longsight retorts. "She embedded the blade into my body. It was not a trick. It was a real dagger, real blood, a real death. My heart stopped. Within minutes, the people knew the truth – their leader was dead. They even laid my body in state, allowing people, over the course of two days, to pay their respects. I was anointed with embalming oil, wrapped in blue cloth – ready for the flayer's blade."

I stare at him and grit my teeth. "But people don't just come back from the dead," I say.

"You're right. People don't." And with that, Mayor Longsight turns and walks on. I glance at Jack and I think I catch him frowning – looking at Longsight, not as though he was Saint reborn or a miracle maker, but as though he were a fool. The look passes before I can process it and I am shoved forward, following Longsight once again.

Chapter Four

We walk on, down steps until we are below ground level. It smells different, as though the air is old. We must be quite deep underground by the time we reach a set of double wooden doors that suggest the start of a new wing – a part of the government building I have never seen before.

Mel, Saintstone's storyteller, has been waiting for us. She nods respectfully to the mayor. Our eyes meet for a second and I feel it all over again – the electric pulse that comes from her, the way she fills a space just by existing. Her red curls are pinned up off her face, and her intricately inked skin reminds me of being read to as a child. Although she intimidates me, she is also the taste of home and with that comes a strange comfort.

"Your new charge," Minnow says to Mel, gesturing to me with a flourish.

"She has not received ink?" Mel asks, her gaze sweeping over me – eyes lingering on my left arm. "Why not? She is a criminal and should be marked as such." I notice Longsight's mouth tighten at being questioned but his voice is light when he replies.

"You fear I will not ensure justice is done? Believe me, storyteller, her punishment will come. For now, though, she is in your charge."

Mel's mouth opens but then she nods assent.

Longsight clasps her arm. "I'm counting on you, Mel. I value your faithfulness."

Mayor Longsight and Minnow turn and walk back through the wooden doors. Mel looks after them for a moment. "You have at least been saved a trip to the jail." She turns and looks at me, her eyes unreadable. "Punishment marks are done within earshot of the cells – it's not a nice sound."

"Is that where Obel is?" I glance towards the dark corridor that must head to the prison.

"If he's still alive, then yes," Mel says, and turns. I can only try to keep up with her brisk pace as she walks further into this underground warren of dark, dank corridors and forbidding closed doors.

Eventually we reach a passageway that is familiar, and I realize we've gone all the way under the town square and have ended up at Mel's study, which is in the basement of the museum. I hadn't realized there was underground access to these places and inwardly curse myself for not paying more attention to the turns we took – maybe I would have been able to find a way out.

I look around her study, at the shelves of books and the worn woven rug. Her desk is messy with papers. This is where I came to be told my results – where I learned that I had been accepted as a trainee at Obel's studio. I visited Mel here when I needed her help and advice, back when I thought she was my mentor and that she cared about me. The last time I was here Mel had a charge – a child called Isolda. I wonder where she is now.

Mel shows me around – points out a door to a small bathroom and another that leads into a tiny bedroom where she sleeps.

"You will sleep here." She points to a mattress and some cushions in the corner. "You'll be comfortable enough."

There are no windows to hint at the time of day and so I try to gauge the hour while I arrange the cushions into somewhere I can sit. Time with Longsight always disorientates me – talking with him could have taken hours or just minutes. I am tired from trudging through the forest with Gull, and it was dawn when we arrived in the town. *Oh, Gull.* I close my eyes and think of her, alone – perhaps in the jail. *Perhaps in the hospital,* a cruel voice whispers. *Or she may be dead.* No. Longsight promised that she would be safe for now. I cling to that thought.

The sound of paper on paper and Mel's sighs and the scratch of a pencil making notes lulls me to sleep.

I dream that it is night, and I hear someone call my name. I run, following the sound, but with each step I am no closer to the voice that is crying out for me to save them. Hands claw at my back and I try harder to run, but I can't evade them, can't wriggle free of their grasp. They are on me, and I turn to see my pursuers. Their skin is grey and peeling away to reveal tiny chinks of light — as though they are broken ceramic lanterns, hiding flames inside. Their fingers grasp and scratch at me like dead branches. I don't know whether to fight or give in; whether to peel away more of their skin to reveal the light or to snuff out their sparks. Where they touch me, my skin recedes into grey too. But I fear there will be no light within me.

My own cry wakes me. "You're a noisy sleeper," Mel says. She pulls a book closer to her on her desk.

I go to the small bathroom and wash my face. While I'm there I lift my top and check my skin. Ever since I was bitten by Fenn's dog back in Featherstone, I've had lingering marks which seem to keep travelling lower. Sure enough, the lines snake across my stomach now, a troubling image determined to appear. I try rubbing them away with a flannel and water, but I know it's useless – I know that like the crow on my chest they'll reveal themselves soon enough. These kinds of marks always do.

The study has a comforting smell. Mel's oiled skin gives up its scent of rose, tea and lavender; the books on the shelves and her desk almost breathe with how often they are opened and are allowed to lie with their faces up to the sky. I sit straighter and watch Mel work.

She is frowning over a skin book, her red curls messy and escaping from their pins. Not the normal kind of skin book, but the skin book of a storyteller. Storytellers have no stories of their own recorded – their books are made up of our community's sacred stories.

Mel must have taken this book from the secret shelves she once showed me. Up a set of steps at the back of the museum is a room you would not notice if you didn't know to look. Had she really trusted me back when she took me into that intimate, holy place? It feels like another world. The storytellers are not named and remembered by their families for their deeds and accomplishments like the rest of us. They have no names along their spines, no family trees or faces – only the imprint of the stories they recorded and recounted. Storytellers of the past huddle together skin to skin on the shelves in that hidden room.

They are unknown by most of the community, but for Mel, they are family and history and home.

We sit there for a time in silence, while she turns the pages and I doze. "Where are you?" she mutters to herself, and I watch as she draws the skin book closer and slowly leafs through its pages again, studying each one with a magnifying glass and a frown. "You must be here somewhere."

I stretch and stand, and Mel looks up.

"Can I help?" I ask. I force a smile. "May as well make myself useful."

Mel raises an eyebrow. "There is an art to this, you know." Then she seems to unbend slightly.

"Which story is it?"

"Pull up a chair." She moves hers slightly so there is space for two at her desk and I find a wooden seat – small and low, made for a child – and drag it over so I am sitting next to Mel looking with her at a storyteller's skin book. I am surprised to see that the story she has been puzzling over is the tale of the Sleeping Princess – a story so familiar that we could probably all recite it before we started school.

"The marks are so different to yours," I exclaim. "Aren't you meant to keep the stories unchanged?" I look at Mel's skin – full of colour. The sleeping princess is on her arm – a tangle of green thorns that reaches up to reveal a girl standing tall over a broken spindle. I see the story of the lovers on her calf; they stand, sun and moon converging. The mark that shows Saint is partly hidden by her skirt, but I see him golden and glorious. Her marks are like ripe fruit, and yet the book on the table before us is black and grey – beautiful, *yes* – but it's only when I really look closely at the skin book that I see any similarity between this illustration of the story and the work on Mel's own skin. Mel gives a wry smile.

"These are the kinds of questions I love and yet rarely get to answer. Yes, the marks *have* changed over the years." She passes a hand tenderly over the page in front of her. "If all the storytellers from every generation met together and recited one of our stories, our voices would be as one. The words would be almost identical – we have a strong and faithful history of passing on and speaking the stories perfectly. But when it comes to our marks, we are free to choose – so long as we reflect the stories accurately."

"Why would you be given that freedom?" I ask. "It doesn't sound like the kind of Saintstone I know."

Mel shakes her head in amusement. "You've become cynical." She sits back, and the tips of her fingers play along the lines of ink on her arm. "A storyteller's job has never been just to get the words right." I raise an eyebrow, but Mel doesn't let me interrupt. "My role is not to simply tell the stories, but to enable the people to truly hear them. I look at the world we find ourselves in and I trust that

23

stories can help us make sense of it – my task is to help our community see how they fit into the stories. The ink on my skin is an interpretation of the stories – a way of telling them for us here now. Isn't that what all our creative pursuits do? Our attempts at art tell the same tales in new ways so that we can make sense of the world around us and the spirit within us."

I lean forward. I feel like I am having lessons again. "What if a storyteller gets it wrong? What if their interpretation is false or they are trying to twist the stories to get what they want?"

"This is why we always go back to the beginning. Our skin books stand as a testimony to the generation we served, but every new storyteller starts in the same way – the same words, the same stories, the same fearsome and holy task." She shrugs. "We just bring something different to it."

"What do you think you have brought to the stories?" I am so curious to know.

She thinks for a while. "When I first began as storyteller I thought I was living in a golden age. There was so much passion and faith and a renewed love for obedience to the teachings of our ancestors."

"You don't feel that way now?" I push for Mel to say more.

She sighs. "Now ... now, I see our people more afraid than ever before – and yet at the same time, more sure of their own righteousness. Perhaps it was always this way. Perhaps I was naïve, or too full of hope to see the cracks."

I stare down at the book in front of her. "Why now?" I ask. "Why are you looking at these old books now?"

Mel stares down too.

"I keep wondering if I've missed something. Something crucial." A furrow appears between her eyebrows. "Throughout our history, when something new or unusual happened, the storytellers have been able to look back at the skin books and see that it was predicted or that it was hidden in the stories all along. All of the major events in our history – the blank resettlement, for instance – have been predicted in some way. Just not..." She taps the table absently. "Just not this."

My heart thumps. "And by *this*, you mean Mayor Longsight's reincarnation?" I ask softly.

She looks perplexed, and my heart goes out to her, briefly. Mel has always believed so strongly in her faith. "There must be a precedent for this – his death and resurrection. It must be here somewhere, in these teachings."

"But you can't find it." It's a relief to hear someone else say it too, to have them voice their bewilderment about the mayor's apparent miracle.

Her troubled eyes meet mine. "Not one story talks about a leader who could defy death in this way."

"But the story of the lovers?" I ask. "His queen calls him back from the dead with her love."

Mel smiles a tiny smile. "You always were a good student, Leora," she concedes. "But no, his was a different resurrection – one that changed him. Remember that although the king was the sun, the story ends with him ruling the underworld – the land of the dead – and their son was the living ruler in his parents' place." She turns a page. "There is no precedent for what our mayor claims." She shakes her head. "Our people will look to me to explain. They need me now, more than ever." She lifts her eyes to mine once more, and where once I saw certainty, now I see only fear. "My training should have prepared me, but my hands are empty."

Chapter Five

There are some things that once shattered can never be put back together again.

Given an egg, do you break it and make something new with the golden innards, or do you simply admire its smooth and perfect shell?

I think about the crack that is appearing now, before my eyes, in Mel's faith. Do I tell her that there are more stories than the ones she knows? Will it make something new? Or would it be better, kinder and more beautiful to let her keep her shell of reality smooth and perfect?

I think of the mark on my foot – the egg with the cracks that let the light in. Breathing deeply, I begin.

"You remember you told the lovers' story at my father's weighing of the soul ceremony?" I venture. Mel nods. "Well – Featherstone have a different version." Mel's eyebrows dip. "It has some of the same things: lovers, a box, a death – of sorts."

"They tell stories?" Mel asks in disbelief.

"Do you think they are savages? Yes, they tell the same stories you do – but each is like a mirror image. The same, but not." Mel frowns and shakes her head. "If you will allow me," I say persuasively, "I think a different story may help you here."

She nods, slowly, and I begin.

Here's one you might not have heard, Sana had said – as though there was something illicit in the sharing. And I feel that rush of rebellion now, as I let my lips form the words.

"The story begins like ours. A king and a queen rule over the people but the king is despised by his brother. But in this story, the king and queen lead with cruelty: leaders who care more for power than their people.

"The king, called Metheus, loves the authority he wields over the people and he hungers for more. And so, under the council of his cunning wife, Metheus holds a banquet where he claims that he is undefeatable. He climbs into a casket, which is flung into the river. The king and queen elaborately fake Metheus' death and when he appears again to the people three days later they are astonished. Their king's boasts were true: he is indeed favoured by the ancestors. He is their immortal leader, and even though he leaves them hungry and works them hard, he must have pleased the ancestors. The people's devotion to their king only grows.

"But one man doubts. The king's brother hears the

queen describing how they tricked the people: the king is no more immortal than him. The brother learns another crucial fact: the king is convinced by his own trickery; he believes he has been resurrected and favoured by the ancestors. He is certain that he will not die.

"And so, Metheus' brother plays a trick. He only means to make a fool of his boastful brother, by holding another banquet and allowing the people to see their king get drunk and make a spectacle of himself. He has not accounted for Metheus' madness.

"The story ends with Metheus slicing at his skin, offering himself up as everlasting food to his people. And the people see that their king Metheus was just a man who believed his own lie and, eventually, came to a sticky, bloody end."

"That's disgusting." Mel's lip curls in revulsion.

"I think it's meant to be a sort of joke," I say gently, and Mel raises her eyebrows disapprovingly. "I think Metheus is meant to be like us – like the marked. When he takes the knife to his own skin, I think the listener is meant to think of skin books and eternal life." As someone who spends so long studying stories, I would have thought she would have seen it right away.

"The blanks think we're fools, then," Mel says bitterly.

"But you see the similarity? A king who dies and comes back to life. Mayor Longsight is just like Metheus."

Mel stares at me. "But ... in that story, it was just a trick. He was never immortal. A cheap trick that the king convinced himself was true."

I say nothing, but I don't take my eyes from her thoughtful, frowning gaze.

Chapter Six

Mel goes to bed early, a notebook and pen in her hand. "My study door doesn't lock, Leora – and I have no desire to stand watch over you all night. If you attempt to escape you *will* be found and you will not be the only one to be punished. Understood?" I nod. I won't try to escape. Now that he has Gull, Longsight has me where he wants me.

Lying on the lumpy cushions, a thin blanket over me, I try not to think about the unlocked door. I try not to think of Gull. I only meant to leave her for a moment.

I try not to think of Mum, and whether what Longsight said was true. She would never turn on me, never. But, lying here in the dark, I imagine her sick and alone and I can see why she despises me. I want to be little again – a young girl who is hemmed in by her mother's love. I am lonely and cold, and no one cares that I am here.

Mel is snoring – not loudly, but once my mind has fixed on it there is no way I can drift off. I tell myself I will just take a walk up and down the corridor – stretch my legs and perhaps tire myself out enough to bring sleep. *I'm a guest, not a prisoner*, I repeat under my breath.

The study door eases open quietly, and outside I feel like I can breathe easier. I walk a little down the corridor – and that's when I see it: light pooling from beneath the door that leads to the museum. . .

I'll just take a look.

I creep up the stairs and emerge behind the reception desk. The stone steps beyond the wide foyer draw me to them – I scamper up, eyes wide, checking each window as I scuttle past. When I peer from the central window at the top of the first set of steps I see a guard out front. I edge away from the window carefully, towards the exhibit of the stories that has been calling to me from the moment I set foot in the museum.

There are ghosts here. Shimmering silhouettes of the past. There is one in my mind's eye whose outline is sharp – my father leading the way, turning his head to smile at me, telling me to *come on, this is the best bit*. Every Saturday it was like the first time he saw the display – his eyes big as a toddler's, his smile wide like someone in love.

Maybe it *was* love – maybe it was his way of seeing her again, in the illustration of the White Witch. Miranda – my birth mother, born in the White Witch's image. She was beautiful, they say. That was part of my story that took a long time to surface – the truth. The truth is messier than fiction. I was born amongst the blanks, and my mother was driven out for loving a marked man.

I stand in front of the White Witch now and wish I had known my birth mother, who died so soon after I was born. Moonlight comes through the skylight and she is paler than ever. I wonder that I never noticed the similarity until Obel made me draw the White Witch that day in his studio. It was like drawing a self-portrait without a mirror. And Obel told me that my mother was even more like her.

I've only known one mother – my mum, stern and quiet with a love for me that I truly thought I could never run too far from. She is the mum I miss, the one whose embrace and forgiveness I am longing for – to me she means safety, she means home. And Dad loved them both. I can't imagine what it must be like to have loved two people in the way Dad loved my mothers. Did the memories overlap? Did he miss the kisses of the one even while savouring the caress of the other?

I press my hand to the glass and another ghost appears. Oscar, his hand next to mine when we barely knew one another. I wish I could go back to that moment. I wish I could go back just a few days, even. Would I have done things differently if I had known that our farewell might be for ever?

My hand clenches into a fist and I want to slam it through the glass. These stories – these tales we have been told – *they're* the problem. We fight, blank and marked, over which sister, which lovers, which saint – if we could just be rid of them all, our fights would be over. I wish I could visit those sisters like I have in my dreams. I would hold their hands and tell them what a mess they've made, beg them to unite once more.

Because that's what I'm here for, so they say. I *am* the sisters; I am them both, Moriah and the White Witch – a bridge, a lifeline, a rope across perilous waters. I went to Featherstone thinking I might be a light to them – that I could guide them back to the truth – Saintstone's truth. But now I know them; I've met the blanks and they are not walking in darkness. They are not blinded to the truth. They have plenty of truth of their own – they are awash with it. It's just that it's not our truth. And the idea of the two coming together is like mixing water and electricity. A storm is brewing, and when the spark of lightning hits the ground, there will be fire.

Chapter Seven

The cold of the stone floor rises through my legs and my feet stiffen, threatening to cramp. I need to get back. But, as I pass the front window, movement outside catches my attention. I stand, back to the wall, peering across my shoulder out of the window in a way that hides me in the darkness as completely as possible. The guard has been joined by another person — a person whose shape and gait has become synonymous with danger to me. Jack Minnow is talking to a guard; he passes him something and then dismisses him.

He watches as the man leaves and for a few quiet minutes he is still and alert. I feel surprised that Minnow takes a watch; I would have imagined standing guard at the museum would be a job for his lackeys — a role far beneath his station. He does love to be in control, though. I am about to resume my return to the study when Minnow looks left and right and then moves. I watch as he passes swiftly across the square. With another glance around, he disappears into the hall of remembrance – the place where our town's readers take turns to speak the names of the dead.

There's no rule against it – the names are spoken constantly, and the hall is always open for mourners and worshippers. But visiting the hall in the dead of night is unusual practice, even for the most devout. For some reason, Jack Minnow needed this action to be secret, and whatever he is doing is worth risking leaving the museum – and me – unguarded.

A person with secrets is a person with vulnerabilities. I tuck this information away in my mind, and once I am back in Mel's study I sleep and dream about a cat and mouse in a maze, only this time, the mouse is chasing the cat.

Chapter Eight

I am woken at dawn by Mel. She looks as though she has dressed in a hurry.

"You have been sent for," she tells me.

"So soon?" I rub my eyes and stifle a yawn.

Mel nods. "We will eat a quick breakfast and then go."

I wish that we would walk through the museum and across the square – I had been hoping for that quick lick of sunlight. Instead, we go through the door at the near end of the corridor, through the underground passage that lies beneath the town square and leads to the prison. As we walk through the cold tunnel I think of Saint and the statue that stands somewhere above us. I imagine being crushed by Saint's heavy bronze feet. The heroes of my past now loom over me nightmarishly. And I know about nightmares.

Jack Minnow waits at the entrance to the jail. His posture reflects his face – confident, assured and superior. *What were you doing last night?* I think. He doesn't speak, just opens the door and we follow.

It is clear that today I will have to visit the prison.

Guards let us in through heavy, locked doors, and with each new corridor, the sense that we are walking further away from light and hope increases. Finally, we reach the cells. They are cave-like and dark – there is no privacy, just a gloomy space cut off by bars. Some cells have two or three people sharing them. No one makes eye contact with us as we pass.

This place exudes absolute loss of hope – all these lives, all this potential, has been locked away and left to decay. At the end of the passage there are more doors – through to private rooms, perhaps interrogation cells. The final open-fronted cell we come to is darker than the rest. This is the corner of hell, where no light or colour can exist.

Jack Minnow stops and peers into the cell.

"Not hiding, I hope, inker?" he taunts. "Come forward and be seen." A scuffling and a groan and the shadow of movement. Obel. He comes crawling, with his eyes screwed up against the pitiful light.

Obel is like an angel whose feathers have been plucked. His hair is longer, brown and straggly. He stinks, and his lips are dry and cracked. The arms that once flexed with power when holding the machine are gaunt and grey. Everything is grey.

Every bright and beautiful colour, every word, every shape and image has faded like a flower that was picked and allowed to slowly die. All his marks are wearing away, the blank spaces spreading like a forest fire.

And when I look closer at the hand that used to create worlds – the one that was crushed by Minnow's rage – I see the fingers that have not been set, the bruising which has become a permanent swelling and the scar that is red and blue as though showing the rage that broke it. There are new marks too – not ink, but a catalogue of bruising in all its miserable shades. Obel, my Obel, is broken. And his skin tells it all.

Down on my knees, I reach out my hands to him through the bars and he lets me hold him.

"You were meant to run." There is a scratch to his voice – thirst or the result of screams, I don't know. He sounds bewildered, confused and small. It feels as though something within him has been replaced by a child whose soul doesn't fit right inside his skin.

"I'm safe." I whisper into his ear – not knowing whether it's true or not, but he needs some hope. "And I'm going to help you." Another promise I have no means of keeping. But I can't tell him the truth; that I am as helpless as he is.

Obel tries to stand, hauling himself up. He is weak. I force myself to look at him again, to take in the full horror of how changed he is, how beaten down. Dread shivers through me – I can't let this happen to Gull. I look around, as though I will find an escape route or a way forward, but of course, all I see are bars and locked doors.

I catch a glimpse, then, of Connor Drew, Oscar's father, in a nearby cell. I haven't seen him since that day – a day that feels as though it was years ago even though it was only last autumn. That day he was publicly marked with a crow – and watching him be branded so cruelly brought back old and buried memories of my dad and his matching mark of the forgotten. Our eyes meet, and he nods. I remember Oscar saying that his father had told him about me. He was the one who tried to help my dad by hiding the illicit mark.

The sound of footsteps breaks our connection and a man wearing all black approaches.

"Jack Minnow looks at me. "I didn't just bring you down here for an emotional reunion. There is work to be done."

Jack Minnow seems to fill up with life on seeing how empty Obel is. He positively glows down here in the dark. A parasite who feeds on misery.

Obel stares, barely blinking at the ground. His every breath seems to squeeze his body of energy. Even in the half-light I see Minnow's eyes gleam with pleasure, seeing what he has done to diminish this man.

"I need you to make him presentable." Minnow turns to me and smiles snakily. "Clean him up and get those *marks* painted on him again. I don't care how you do it, just get it done. You have three days." I stare at Obel, confused, then turn back to Minnow. He smiles. "Come on, inker. Show us how good you really are."

And with that, he is gone. Mel is bewildered too, I can tell – she stares after him, confusion written on her face. Minutes later a prison guard comes with food – good food, not prison slop.

"I will return at the end of the day," Mel tells me. She seems as though she wants to say more – to stay, even – but then she shakes her head and leaves. The guard opens the cell door and I go into the den, hoping that I can make Obel ready in time.

In time for what, I have no idea.

I call for hot water, for clean linen, for oils.

I bathe Obel's skin.

Skin. It's become a theme to my life.

Rubbing oil into Dad's weak arms when he was dying – letting the ink that covered his wasted wrinkles gleam.

The feeling of Oscar's hand that first day we met – his fingers on mine, gripping me tight, taking me with him, away from the questions at the museum. Drinking coffee together in the little coffee house, windows fogged up, trying to dance round each other's words to know how much of our true selves we could show.

Stop it. Don't think of him.

I remember the first mark I made, under Obel's watchful eye. I loved the click and buzz of the machine in my hand as I held that pale woman's skin taut with my left hand and inked into it with my right. A leaf for a baby. A forbidden mark for a lost life. Obel condoning it. Drawing me in. Into his web of rebellion, hoping I would help him weave it into something wonderful.

Broken ceramic slicing across my hand; blood in the washing-up water.

Gull's skin bubbling in agony as she tried to mark it with dust and ash.

Karl's strong hand pulling me to face him as we argued, his fingers digging in to my shoulder as I slipped and fell.

The smell of lavender as Mum bathed my tender skin.

The marks that grew alone, telling me my story before I understood what it would be.

I think of these things as I work so that I don't think about Obel.

I tend to him as though he is a customer at the studio, a stranger. It is like when Dad was ill: losing him bit by bit, seeing him become watered down until all we had was diluted – a hint of him, a memory of a flavour.

But this is different; Obel is not dying. Over two long days I wipe decay from his skin and feed him with water and bread, sips of beer and slices of apple. And as the grime is rinsed away, I think I begin to see him emerge. His back straightens, his teeth bite the apple and the juice drips from his chin. Shoulders back, eyes clear, and with a sigh I hear the whisper of my name. I smile grimly. *How's this for a resurrection, Longsight?*

The guards bring me balm for Obel's sore skin, clippers for his nails, and clean clothes for him to wear.

On the second day, I ask him why he is still here. What purpose he is going to serve.

"I don't know," he mutters. "No idea."

Connor Drew laughs then, a harsh sound in the inky dark. "Don't play ignorant, Obel," he calls out. "Why would Longsight keep an inker under lock and key? An inker who is utterly at his command, who can be made to do whatever the mayor demands?"

He comes forward and leans against the bars. Underneath the grime and stubble, I think I can see Oscar in his face. I look away. "What does Longsight want, then?" I ask them both, trying to keep my tone gentle, attempting to hide the fear and dread. "Why does he want you cleaned up and marked again? Obel – what's going on?"

Obel only glares at Connor.

"It's not over yet. You're a fighter," I murmur and rub balm into his right hand. The bones have set crooked, leaving his fingers splayed and weak – I ask him to move them, to grip my hand, and he turns his head away. His fingers shake as he attempts to make a fist – his fingertips don't even reach his palm.

"We need to get this reset," I tell him. It feels oddly maternal to be handling him in this way, and I think of his mother, Tanya, back in Featherstone, and how this would break her heart. She has lost both Obel and Gull.

I wonder again where Gull is. She must be alive – she must be. Longsight said she would be safe.

Because if she isn't, then it's all my fault.

Later that day I take up scissors and start cutting his hair. When I first met Obel his hair was shaved, then he let it grow to a neat crop, but now it's a straggly, matted mess.

I know I am doing it badly – too short over the ears, raggedly cut over his eyes. But I carry on cutting, snipping away the tangles.

"He wants me to mark you," I tell Obel. "To paint you like you were before. Why?"

"Because he wants a public marking." I almost drop the scissors in shock, but Obel raises a hand. "Oh, not for me – he wants me to make the mark. I don't know who will be marked, with what or why. A new teaching, he said. He will – what was it – 'take the people's pain away'." He shrugs. "I'll do as I'm told."

"Obel," I chide. I hate the defeated tone of his voice. It scares me – like he has lost enough hope to make him reckless. It both frightens me and thrills me. I want to be brave. I will make my own armour and fight by his side. If only I knew what the war was.

Obel and I are sitting next to each other, leaning against the stone wall of his cell, when Mel comes to collect me. I've done enough today – tomorrow is for marks and I can only hope his skin settles well enough overnight for the inks to go on smoothly and cover the gaps.

That night, I wander the museum again, and again I see Jack Minnow and watch as he treads guiltily towards the hall of remembrance. No one is so faithful as to visit the hall every night, and especially not Jack Minnow

Whatever he is hiding in these night-time shadows, I will bring to light.

Chapter Nine

I dream about Oscar — dream that he is on a hospital trolley. The nurses shake their heads and tell me he is gone, and they pull the sheet up over his face. I shout and draw back the cotton cover and his face is a mask — a mask only. I tear it off and beneath the mask is a grinning Sana.

"Dead? Alive? It makes no difference in Featherstone." She smiles a horrible smile. "Join me, Leora. Take my hand and walk with me." And she towers over me, a giant — a monster. A warrior. She holds out her hand to me.

I reach out.

I wake before I see what happens next — whether or not our hands touch. I don't go back to sleep after that. I just wait for dawn, letting my mind paint Obel's marks over and again. I will make him perfect.

Obel is a different man when I go to him on the third day. He is himself again, somehow. The dignity of being clean. Guards have already brought the dyes and inks, brushes of all sizes, and he eats his breakfast quickly, keen to get started. I feel relief start to creep back in. I recognize this Obel.

Like I do when I'm inking with a machine, I begin with the lines. Some, I trace over the faded marks that still show on Obel's skin, but in other places I rely on memory and Obel's guidance.

"Keep the linework clean, Leora," he tells me, watching carefully, ever my teacher. "Make sure the swallow is – no, a bit higher than that – so it moves with the muscle. Yes, good." He's desperate to do this himself, I can tell, but his wings are clipped. He has to rely on me.

Painting skin is nothing like inking. I have to consciously remind myself not to instinctively wipe with every pause of the brush, as I would with needles and ink. I have to learn a new language of skin and resistance and softness. There is no blood. There is no pain. And I miss it, that bite of pain inflicted. I miss knowing I am doing deep work, a mark which means more because with every gasp, every bitten lip and sigh, the person lives their ink – earns it. It's the pain that makes it matter. The swelling as your body fights against the intrusion, the brightly coloured scabs, the sting of remembering your mark when you run your newly inked arm across the edge of a table or pull on your coat too roughly. What is the tickle of a brush and dye that will dry in an instant? You have not earned those stripes.

But Obel – he's earned something. He deserves more than this.

Chapter Ten

Mel insists on braiding my hair before we go out. She pulls the strands tight. She says it's to make me look presentable, but when I ask, "Presentable for what?" she just braids faster. Her hands shake. Our three days are up, and today I get to discover what Obel's rehabilitation has all been about.

I have been provided with new clothes – nothing showy, not like Mel's uniform of gilded metal and leather which looks so beautiful on her lush flesh and rounded body. I am clean and neat, and I get the impression that I am being dressed in such a way as to make sure I don't stand out. That's fine by me.

It is still early when I put the finishing touches to Obel's skin and follow Mel and three guards as they lead the way through the warren of tunnels towards the government building. An official joins us and when I turn my head I almost gasp. It's Karl – Karl Novak, my nemesis from the studio; Karl who laid his hands on me in a moment of rage.

But also – Karl, who tried to warn me before Dad's soul-weighing. Our eyes meet; he gives the merest shake of his head to warn me not to acknowledge him and I look back at the ground. He's made his way up the ranks swiftly to be entrusted with criminals like us.

I scan each corridor we walk down for Verity. The last time we spoke it felt like an ending – the end of a friendship that had been my anchor through life. Do we still love each other – or do we hate each other now? She was Longsight's messenger, all the time I was in Featherstone. She hated how I came to speak of the blanks with compassion. And I hated hearing her admiration for the mayor. When we parted ways that last time, it split us in two.

We wait near the wide doors that lead to the square. Obel's hands are cuffed behind him and I see the fingers of his left hand clench and release, as though he is warming up for a fight. His broken right hand simply hangs there.

Why has Longsight chosen him for this? The finest inker once, but now unable to hold a needle. Why not one of the government inkers?

My thoughts are interrupted by the sound of music and cheers – a festive atmosphere has already been set. The sun is bright, and the sky is cloudless blue. Only a week ago, Mayor Longsight brought me out and paraded me as the spoils of battle – moments later he was covered in his own blood. *And then he rose again, remember?* says a little voice in my head, and I shiver. A trick, I tell myself. But how?

Jack Minnow arrives and stands at Obel's side and I wish I knew what his secret was. He is too strong, and I am too afraid.

When the mayor arrives, surrounded by bodyguards, the doors are opened, and the cries of the crowd almost knock me back. A stage has been erected, huge speakers stand at the sides and swathes of deep red velvet cover every visible surface. This is going to be something big.

Mayor Longsight is led out by his guards with Jack Minnow at his heels. Meanwhile, Obel, Mel and I are pulled to a side door by Karl and the three guards. We emerge, blinking, in the bright sunlight behind the stage. We are hidden from the eyes of the crowd, but we have the best seats for the spectacle. I won't miss a thing, even if I want to.

Jack Minnow steps up to the microphone which is front and centre of the stage. He calls for quiet.

"People of Saintstone – it has only been a short while since everything changed." His dark eyes survey the crowd. "Since the miracle." There is a sort of collective gasp from the crowd – a miracle is how they see it. "You must have questions. And now our leader is here to answer them. Prepare your hearts and minds for a new message – the new word from our exalted mayor, the only man to triumph over death."

The roar from the crowd makes me draw back. The people of Saintstone have always been in Mayor Longsight's thrall, but this is something new. It is adoration, wild worship. He has become their saviour – an incarnate deity. Faces are almost frantic with delight.

And all the time, Mayor Longsight stands statue-tall, soaking up the praise while humbly gesturing for quiet. It is many minutes before the people are calm enough to obey his request, but once he has their attention, they are rapt.

"I have put you through so much," he says. "I can only imagine your fear and horror at seeing your leader assassinated just a short time ago – and in such a shocking and public way." There is another murmur: a swelling, fearful sound. "And yet – and yet, my friends – I live." The murmur turns to cries of joy, and Longsight looks out over the crowd, his expression euphoric. "You have allowed me to live again!" he cries. "The ancestors have spoken to me. It was your faith that they saw, and they have rewarded you. For this is a new era, a time of hope and change and victory."

The crowd erupts once more, and I turn my head to look at Mel. There is a furrow between her eyebrows. If Longsight has been communicating with our ancestors, then she should have been the first person he told.

Mayor Longsight speaks to the people again.

"When I was in the clutches of death I heard a voice – a message so clear and so pure. I have longed to share this new word with you. I have had to show restraint – to wait until the time is right. I have been given a new teaching and it is good news – good news for all."

Mel catches her breath beside me. The mayor waits. The silence swells. "You are all good people," he says at last. "And yet – you all fear the same fate. That, one day, all of your ink will not be enough. That despite all we are taught, all that we know, our sins will catch up with us. Well, what would you say if I could assure you of peace? What if there was a way to absolve you, to atone before you are judged? To offload your sins. Would you believe me? Would you come and partake of this blessed freedom?"

And hope, like a traitor, rises in my chest. A worm wriggling free from a corpse. *Yes*, I think. Some certainty – a map, a guide, a signpost and a clear path. If I could be sure of a way to be remembered for ever, to be certain that my soul was good enough and that there was an eternity ready to embrace it – well, then I would run to that certainty and nail everything I have to it. I see the same hope shining golden in the eyes of each person in the crowd. Hungry mouths open in awe, ready to taste the bounty that Mayor Longsight is holding out to them.

I swallow. Poison can taste like honey, but it will kill you all the same. *Wait and see, Leora*, I tell myself. *Patience*.

"What is it that weighs you down?" Mayor Longsight asks, pausing so long I wonder if he's actually waiting for an answer. "We mark our bodies to free our souls – but don't you feel the weight of the ink that shows your evil, furtive, treacherous ways? Don't you feel it heavy in your veins?" He looks down at his own left arm, empty of punishment marks. I see people in the throng follow suit, looking at their own marks. I let my eyes relax and I read the people closest to me.

The guard at my right has his children's names marked on his bicep; I can see clearly that he is ashamed of his harsh words to his son.

A person at the front of the crowd has jewels inked at her collar bone. They tell me of the time she stole her sister's precious bracelet.

We all have guilt.

I remember Obel telling me how he saw our marks and our lives – not as good or bad, black or white, not even grey, but layers of colour swirling into something uniquely beautiful. But all I see as I look around is kindling for the fire in the hall of judgement. Skins that breathe secret sin. Souls that do not deserve an eternity of remembrance.

Souls not worth saving.

We are guilty. We will be judged. We deserve what we get.

No, Leora, I tell myself, shaking off the stupor he has

sent me into, despite myself. *You are not a tick list of good and bad. Ink does not say it all. It doesn't even say half of it.*

I turn back to the stage. Longsight nods to the wings, and two guards lead a man to the stage – and it is a stage, I must remind myself. This is theatre. The man is slight and quivering with fear. His big, anxious eyes scan the crowd and I see his jaw work nervously. He is ushered forward to stand next to the mayor, who takes a step to the side so that the microphone is between them.

"What is your name?" Longsight asks, his eyes smiling.

"Philip. Ph-Philip Knowles." He leans into the microphone, his wary eyes glancing around.

"You are an inmate of the jail here in Saintstone. So, tell me, Philip Knowles. Tell us all – what have you done?" He says it like a calm teacher to a rebellious child. *What have you done?* "Come, Philip. What brought you here? Tell us."

The man's eyes dart nervously. "I ... I stole from the market stall, and when I was chased and caught, I hit Jonathan Delaney, the grocer. I broke his jaw. He's not been able to work since."

A disapproving murmur from the crowd. We don't like violence in Saintstone.

"My daughter was ill, you see," the man tries desperately to explain. "I have had to care for her – I couldn't work. We don't have anything. I never meant..."

The man's attempt at justification is lost in the jeers of the watching people. Saintstone is not sympathetic to those who can't work, who can't pay their way, who aren't useful.

"What does our man Knowles deserve?" Mayor Longsight puts it to the people, as though this is a pantomime or a magic show.

Voices rise – some call for "Ink! Ink! Ink!": a thick red line, the mark due for violent theft. But I also hear the word I dread: "Crow." They want him not just marked, but forgotten. It sounds like a howl – like the bay of dogs.

Longsight smiles, and raises his hands. "Those of you calling for the crow – I ask you, do not forget mercy." He says it like they are overexcited children that he must reluctantly chide rather than grown men and women who have called for this man's soul to be obliterated. "But, you are right – a sin cannot go unpunished." Longsight is speaking slowly and clearly; the sound calms the crowd and they hush, ready to listen to his verdict, holding back their eager cheers. "But what if there was a way for this sin to be punished and yet at the same time for this man to be unmarked? For him to experience atonement, forgiveness, freedom?"

I frown then, because what Longsight is talking about is impossible. Unless this man is marked, unless the sin is written on the body, then there is no way he can be free.

Next to me, Mel lifts a hand to her open mouth. I wonder what she has seen that I have not.

Two more guards come for Obel then, undoing his cuffs and chivvying him along one at each of his shoulders. His marks look perfect, I notice, with a flicker of professional pride. Anyone who didn't know Obel before would think he was in fine health; only I see the slight stoop in his posture and the weight in his steps.

Obel is escorted up the steps to the stage by Jack Minnow. All the inking paraphernalia is set up: two seats – a stool for Obel, and another chair. There is a workstation ready to be used. Obel sits on the stool, looking calmly out at the crowd.

The prisoner begins to weep.

Obel gives Minnow a little nod to show that he is ready, and Mayor Longsight steps to the microphone again and addresses his prisoner.

"Mr Knowles. Do you admit your guilt?"

The man answers. "Yes, Mayor Longsight. I admit my guilt." The words sigh from him, almost inaudible.

"And you agree that your actions deserve – indeed, require – punishment?"

"I do," he murmurs, but his quiet voice can't hide from the microphone and he has called punishment down himself, in front of us all.

"Do you trust in me, Philip Knowles?"

A strange question. And, bravely, I think, Philip Knowles pauses.

People shift their feet and cough, unnerved by the silence.

"I . . . I do trust you Mayor Longsight." And there is steel in those words. One of Mayor Longsight's eyebrows flickers.

"A wise answer." Mayor Longsight smiles enigmatically. "Now, Philip. Do you *worship* me?"

The man is silent, but the crowd cheers and that is enough for Longsight.

"If a man could bear your sorrows. If a man could take on your guilt, because he himself had pleased the ancestors where you could not. If a man could be marked in your place, the ink on his skin, your sin in his blood. If a man could do all this. *Then*, would you worship him?"

The roar from the crowd is terrifyingly loud – the stage rocks with the stamps of the joyous people and my ears ring with their screams of praise.

Yes. A man like that, they would worship.

Chapter Eleven

Jack Minnow steps to the fore.

"People of Saintstone, I call on you to witness and to pass on what you see. You will tell your children, and they will tell their children of this day."

Phillip Knowles is jostled to the side of the stage as robes of scarlet are brought to the mayor and slipped on over his bare skin. A crown of red roses is placed on Longsight's head as he is led to the chair. Petals flutter to the ground as he walks, to be crushed underfoot.

The drape of the robes as he sits on the chair before Obel reminds me of water cascading – rivers of blood. He gathers the fabric so that the mayor's left arm is fully exposed; Obel shifts his stool closer. I see him reach for a razor. He's preparing the skin; he's really doing this.

Jack Minnow anoints his leader's feet with perfumed oil and the kneeling crowd rises.

The machine whirrs to life with its insect-shrill sound and Obel dips the needle into the ink. He holds

Longsight's arm still, his skin taught. He's managing, despite his broken hand. I hear the higher pitch as needle attacks skin and the hitch of Mayor Longsight's breath as he submits to the bite.

The line that emerges is wide and red. The mark of a thief.

I breathe deeply and inhale the fragrance of petals blending with richly scented oil. The air is heavy and seductive. The machine stutters to silence. I know what will happen next – Obel's routine never changes. He will clean, cover and dress the mark. After a moment, when Obel releases him, Mayor Longsight stands, bidding his people to stand with him.

They see his forearm, bound in transparent film. They smell the oil and crushed flowers and they praise him. Their leader – one who sits in the seat of punishment and takes it upon himself. This is a new day, a new teaching, a new era.

Chapter Twelve

"What's he going to do now?" I say sourly when Mel and I reach her study. "Get a mark for every sneak thief in the jail?"

I'm playing down my shock. Despite myself, I was stunned out there. Longsight took a mark for another. Took on that man's sin. But now, back in Mel's office, I feel my cynicism kicking in. Whatever that was today, it was for show. Longsight might believe himself immortal, but he's pragmatic. There are reasons for the charade and they will be reasons that somehow benefit him.

Mel sits at her desk in silence – she must hear me but it's as though she has learned to turn my volume down. She stares into space, hand resting on her marbled notebook. She looks like she's waiting for something. Long minutes pass and she appears to come to, her eyes sharply focused on me.

"That story. . ." she says. "The one you told me about the king, Metheus. . ."

I nod.

"You said there were more. More blank stories." Her expression is at once expectant and nervous.

"Why do you want to know?" It's not like Mel to ask questions – she always has all the answers. I am angry with her, suddenly. "I thought you knew everything." She watches me quietly, a small smile on her lips. "Why should I trust you with their stories?" I ask.

"There is much that I do not know, Leora Flint; I admit that." She looks at me coolly. "The beginning of wisdom is realizing just that – that there is so much more to the world than you can ever know or understand." She runs her hand through her curls, and her smile becomes mocking. "You, though – you go on one journey and you think you are an expert. You are like a feather – you think you are free but instead you are at the whim of the wind. Do not speak to me about knowledge or fear, truth or faith. Your head is turned by a good story, a warm fire, a smile, a handsome face. You flit from friend to friend and wonder why you have none left."

In the silence that follows, I see her face soften.

"I like you. I like what I see in you. I still do. You gave me hope. I said you were special and I believed— *believe* it. But you have to act, now. I have reached the end of my own knowledge. I am a seeker of truth and I need your help." She leans forward. Her face is flushed. "Share their stories with me," she says softly. "I think it might be important."

And so it is in this small room, Mel at her desk and me sat on cushions, that I open the covers of the book that is in my mind and the storyteller becomes the listener.

"In a wood, near a village, there was a woodcutter's house. . ."

Chapter Thirteen

I tell Mel the stories she already knows, but from a new vantage point. The story of the sisters, who grew up in the wood, and how one became a princess and the other went into exile. Only this time the twin with the ink was the wicked one. The lovers – all the more shocking a second time in the telling. Nate – a new perspective on Saint, a spy rather than a saviour. The sleeping princess who broke free from her parents' oppression and broke down the walls that surrounded her. The gift given to brothers who had no idea of the trickster's heart.

Mel pours tea from a tall pot and lets an amber globule of honey melt into each cup before stirring.

"It's good for the voice," she tells me as she hands me a cup.

I've been talking a long time, and as I told her those precious stories I felt a warm possessiveness which unfolded into generosity – a desire to protect the tales by telling them well. The way Mel closed her eyes as she listened, smiled and nodded when the story resonated, wiped away tears – she made it holy, accepting the delicate, fragile stories as only a true storyteller could.

We sip tea in silence, the words still bobbing in an ocean of story between us.

After we have drunk the final drops, Mel places her notebook and pen carefully in a drawer and locks it. She stands.

"Come." She reaches a hand out to me down on the cushions. "There's something I want you to see."

When we reach the bottom of the private staircase I know where we are going: to see the skin books of the storytellers. The door opens with a held-breath gasp, as though it has too few visitors. The fragrance of these old skin books is a close, heavy scent that makes the air feel warm. These are the skin books of the storytellers, saved for ever. Our community needs stories and must remember them – they must be handed down immaculately.

Our storytellers learn the tales and speak them word-perfect to the people. More than this though, they wear the stories – their skin is a homage to our history. It's always the same stories. We must not forget them.

I've been in this room once before, when Mel was still my mentor, when she still saw potential in me. When she had plans for my future. She had run her hands over the spines of the books in meditative delight. I remember thinking how sad it was that this was all she would have to show for herself when she died – the marks of stories that were not her own. Even then the cracks in my belief were beginning to show.

Now, though, Mel pauses by one of the bookcases, crouches down, and presses at its base. A drawer springs out. She reaches in and takes out a wooden box.

"You will want to touch," she tells me. "Do not."

Undoing the metal clasp, Mel lifts the lid and lets it rest open on its hinged edge. With great care she removes a rectangle of linen and steps aside, so I can see more clearly the item she has revealed.

Skin.

A piece of skin about the size of the palm of my hand. Its edges curl, looking frayed and irregular and showing signs of where it was pegged out to dry. Mel was right – I am desperate to touch it. It looks different from our skin books – thicker and more brittle. If I did touch it, I think, it would feel crisp and rough. I lean in and Mel puts a protective hand on the side of the box. I see hairs, and, on the skin where they grow are goosebumps – as though caught mid-shiver. This has not been tanned in the way our skin books are – the lye removes hair and evens out the surface. This is rudimentary – either due to age or lack of care.

But the biggest shock of all is the mark itself.

Because I've seen it before.

I look down at my stomach, as though the fragment of skin has made me transparent. If Mel could see my torso, then she would have seen a crisp, traced outline of the mark I see before me now.

Two women, face to face, hands clasped.

The sisters.

I've seen them in my dreams. Their faces are alike – they are twins after all – but their bodies are night and day. Moriah and Belia, the sisters whose divergent journeys are the paths we have followed ever since, one people marked like Moriah and another blank like Belia. Each woman is a queen to her followers and accursed to her enemies. When I dream of them, they are always so sad. But those are just dreams.

"When this was found, by all accounts, it caused quite a storm." Mel smiles but her eyes are anxious.

"What does it mean?" I ask.

"It's a symbol of the sisters reunited. After everything – after Moriah is utterly covered in ink and the White Witch—"

"Belia," I interrupt. "Her name is Belia."

"*Belia. . .*" Mel says, "is utterly blank and bare. And yet, this image seems to depict an idea that at the end – towards the end of their lives and reigns – the sisters came back together. Perhaps even reconciled."

"It's incredible," I whisper. My fingers itch to be able to touch – just once. "You think this was part of a skin book?"

"I do, but a very old one. Some storytellers argue that it is the skin of a storyteller who was alive in the time of Moriah. They believe that this is the final story that storyteller told. There is another theory, fanciful though it may be," ventures Mel. Her voice is deliberately light. "Some past storytellers have argued that this is the skin of Moriah herself – that this was her final message to her people."

I stare at her. "A message – a declaration," I breathe. "A record claiming that the sisters had reconciled in the past – and that blank and marked could do so again. . ."

Mel watches me, her blue eyes hooded.

"But if the sisters had reconciled," I go on, thinking aloud, "then surely that would be widely known? People wouldn't live like this if there was a better way. . ."

But even as I say that, I think of Sana – Sana, who starved her own people to make them more likely to fight. Jack Minnow, whose eyes light up when he sees violence. Even if they were given every reason, every chance for peace, I think that people would still choose war.

"Whose skin do *you* think it is?" I ask Mel.

Her voice as she replies is dreamy. "In my wildest thoughts I have hoped that this might be the skin of Belia."

I stare at her in surprise, and she shrugs. "That she came back. That she repented and was marked and rejoined her sister, living under Moriah's good rule."

"Is that what you want for the blanks?" I ask. "Even now?"

"I pray for their repentance," she says, nodding. "That they find hope." I'm surprised to feel a lump in my throat.

"The blanks have hope," I say. And I think of the stones, the lake and Fenn's face when he came up from the water. I remember the day Ruth died and their voices soaring high, sending her soul on its final journey. That was real – as real as this. "They have faith, too. It's just different to the stories we know. Not wrong. Just different."

"I'm beginning to think you might be right, Leora." Mel closes the box, biting her lip as she tucks it back into its hidden compartment. "And when I think of what that might mean for me and my people, it terrifies me."

Chapter Fourteen

While I wait for the dead of night, that moment when everyone but you is asleep and the world cannot get more silent, I think of Jack Minnow. I want to know what he does each night in the hall of remembrance.

I slip out of Mel's study, closing the door with as little sound as possible, and head for the steps up to the museum. Mel stayed up late, a thin crack of light visible under her door, but eventually she had gone to sleep.

I reach the reception area. Lights from the town square cast a dim glow across the entrance way. I rattle the doors experimentally, but they are of course locked. I go through the drawers, looking for anything of use, but there is nothing. As I shut one, I knock over a pen pot and hold back a laugh when I see it among the pencil sharpenings: a key.

I hold it in my palm, examining it closely. It is silver and decorative. Gazing at the space around me, trying to work out where it might fit, I walk deeper into the building and try the doors to the library, but the key doesn't match. I skirt the edges of the large space and I can feel my hope stretching its arms out.

There is one place left, and it is calling me: behind the green door. I can hardly bear to reach my hand out to the handle because I know what I will see, and I know that since I came here last, the only thing that will have changed is me – and that that changes everything.

The handle is cold. I know the key will fit before I try it. A small twist, a dull click, one deep breath and I turn the handle, pushing the door and pulling my fear into my centre. Dust and stale air dry my throat and I splutter – it feels like a neglected space. But they still bring children here; I see evidence of a recent visit – worksheets and pencils, clipboards and a forgotten hat. Of course they wouldn't stop the school trips to this place – not only is it a rite of passage, it matters more than ever that the children of Saintstone hear this story. They need to be convinced – to be absolutely certain of the threat their enemy poses – because that is the only way. Make your enemy less than human, then make that less-than-human dangerous, *then* make the danger feel close. Easy.

The glass-faced exhibits that edge the room are oppressively dark. I know that behind the shiny exteriors there is a blood-stained knife, a severed hand, a damning letter. Evidence. All here to convince the viewer of their own righteousness in the face of blank wickedness. I am repelled by these dark corners – but the centre of the room scares me even more.

I move closer to the tank and force myself to look.

His was the first dead body I ever saw. The man who floats here in the eerily glowing water used to terrify me – because he was proof. Proof of blanks and our victory. I never thought of his life or of the story of his death. He was a symbol – a deterrent and nothing more. Beware the blanks.

I reach out my hands, touch the glass. Tears fall without my realizing. Rain on windows. I wonder – can he hear the *tap, tap, tap*?

He could be any of them: Fenn, Solomon, Tanya, Gull. He was just a man with no marks and we made him a monster. We boast about not fearing death and yet we relished the horror that this man's death made us feel. I remember we would lean on this tank as though it were a table. We'd fill out our worksheets, chat and bite the ends of our pencils, all the time treating this man's grave as little more than a piece of furniture – a thing unremarkable save for its usefulness to us at that moment. My chest heaves and I whisper to this unnamed soul that I am sorry.

Standing here, I remember something, something from those long-ago school visits, and as if in a dream I walk to the thick, black curtain in the corner. I can remember our teachers would always tell us about the escape route in case of a fire.

The fire escape door is there, as I knew it would be. It is locked from the inside by a bolt which slides effortlessly even though my fingers shake. I open the door a chink, and movement catches my attention.

You can sense a spider out of the corner of your eye just from the shape of its movement.

That is how I feel about Jack Minnow. I loathe him, and yet I know him. I know how he moves. He makes me want to run, to retreat, to hide; but he also draws me to him. He intrigues me. Isn't that how some predators work? They lure you on, even while your mind screams at you to run. But for now, I have the power, because he doesn't know I'm here. I watch him hurry into the hall of remembrance, and then follow him. This is my turf.

In Saintstone they believe that so long as someone still says your name, then you are not forgotten. As a reader, Mum was entrusted with the reading of the names in the hall of remembrance. There is a tightening in my chest when I pass the threshold; she might be here tonight. But whatever I see, I must stay quiet. I am here as a shadow and no more – it is the only way.

Mum would sometimes take me along with her to the reading of the names when she was on duty. Some days I loved it, the sleepy magic of it – other days I was bored.

I wanted to stay at home and play. Those hours of having to be quiet and unobtrusive have served me well, though. People come to the reading of the names to hear particular people's names spoken or to light a candle or fulfil an oath. It would not do for a child to disturb their time of reflection. It meant that I learned to pass the time quietly and to find the darkest corners in which to settle myself in order to draw or play. You don't forget the great hiding places from childhood – you only grow too big to fit in them.

I glance unseen into the hall of remembrance and see the readers murmuring the names – a gentle rhythm of plosive and assonance that has, more than once, lulled me to sleep. I see Minnow, sitting towards the back, hunched forward, elbows on knees in the common pose of the worshipper at the hall of remembrance.

I slip in quietly, edging closer and closer to him. The seats are wooden blocks, individual stools rather than the long benches in the hall of judgement. When we mourn we mourn alone – no one can truly share in our sorrow. I know that the stools at the back of the room are piled in columns and tight rows, extra seats in case of a busy day – I've never seen them used. They provide a place for me to stand unseen, to watch and listen. It's easy to tune out the voices of the readers as they list name after name – soon they are just a background buzz. I lean forward, because Minnow's lips are moving. I lean forward, and I listen.

Relax, I tell myself. Stop listening to your own heart hammering. And soon enough it comes to me – the voice of a man at the end of his tether. The sound of a soul that has given up hope. His prayer is simple; two words over and over.

"Davey Minnow."

A name I don't know whispered in the hall of remembrance. A brother? A son? A father?

I remember their faces when I read from my own book – my own paper with names on it:

Connor Drew. Mel. My birth mother, Miranda Flint, and my father, Joel Flint.

I spoke the names that day, the day I renounced Saintstone. Spoke the names that had been wiped from the book of life – names of those not considered worthy, those who didn't belong, those who were supposed to be forgotten. I walked out of this room with my head held high, showing my cloak of ink – feeling ready to soar with that crow as I left their gasps and shouts behind. Angriest of all was Jack Minnow.

And yet here he is, whispering in the dark.

Some animal instinct tells him that I am here. He lifts his head as though he can sense me. There is no time to think; I keep my head covered and bolt for the door. Heavy footsteps behind me tell me that he is following, but I am quicker – I hear him stumble over stools and knock them down. I sprint with everything I've got across the square towards the door.

I reach the door and glance behind me; Minnow has just passed the statue of Saint. I stop, and he does too. We are frozen. Like a magnet repelling us – he can come no closer.

He has seen me, but I saw him too. I heard him.

We each have each other's secrets in our pockets, ready to draw them out at the right moment. I won't hold back. But I will wait.

Who is Davey Minnow?

Chapter Fifteen

In my dream I am a bird.

No, in my dream I am two birds. First a crow, all green-black gloss and intelligent poise. Later I am a magpie, clean-striped and cunning.

As the crow and as the magpie, I flit from tree to tree, checking all the time that my quarry has eyes only for me. I drop leaves, stones and seeds at her feet. I will do my job; I will lure her on.

The one with dark hair knows this game — we have played it before. I, the crow, drop a white stone ahead on the path and she follows my trail. She eyes me with amused suspicion; she is not sure whether we are old friends or enemies. I have no such confusion, for I know that I am neither — I am a messenger. Some call me the bringer of death, a harbinger of sadness. To them, I am only an omen. They don't know me at all. For I am the wise; I am the view from the treetops; I am the guide that leads you to something new.

They call me one for sorrow, but she is the broken one who looks like her body could shatter. All those lines, like fractures.

I, the magpie, must draw her and protect her on this journey. I use my clear voice to call her on. The leaves offer her feet a carpet of gold, finer than any royal furnishing. I, like her, have an eye for jewels and I know how to capture her heart. I am not sorrow, I am love, and if she will just follow me she will find love that never ends.

The mark on my stomach, the mark of the reunited sisters, has darkened overnight, I'm sure of it.

I run my hands across it and think of Moriah – she was the one whose skin grew ink of its own. By rights I should be more like Belia, because by blood and birth I am blank – my mother was blank, and I was born in Featherstone. But I was born marked; my name was written on my skin before any hand touched me. I was a curse, a threat, a warning.

Or I was a saviour. It just depends on whose story is being told. It depends on who is listening.

Mel doesn't wait for me to sit down before she speaks. I can tell from the speed at which she talks – slow, careful, considered – that she has been wanting to say this for a while, she just couldn't decide how.

"What do you know about automatic writing?" she asks as I sit.

I stare at her.

"Right." Mel smiles slightly. "I'll start with a bit of history, then." I wriggle to get comfortable and Mel shifts her chair so it's closer to me. "We talked about how storytellers have had the freedom to choose how the stories are inked on their bodies?" I nod. "Well, these days there is just one storyteller for the town, but once upon a time there used to be a community of storytellers. Like the readers in the hall of remembrance, working together."

"Like Mum," I say.

"Yes, like your mum. The storytellers were a group of scholars, teachers, prophets and mystics. They often were guided by the ancestors to explain or apply a story in a new way for a new time. It was, as far as I can tell from the written records we have preserved, a time of debate and creativity. There were many personalities, many ideas and messages and yet there was also unity; there was freedom and acceptance of differing views. It was a time of rich diversity and the community flourished."

"This doesn't sound like Saintstone," I mutter. "I thought there was only one voice, one way."

She gives me a brief, absent smile. I'm not going to provoke her tonight.

"Well," she goes on, "automatic writing was something that was practiced by those storytellers who were mystics and prophets. They would sometimes go into a trance, or sometimes just be aware that a message was coming, and their hand would write words that their brain had no control over. Their ancestors would speak through them."

I stare at her.

"It sounds dangerous," I say at last. "Anyone could make something up and pretend the ancestors had told them to say it. I'm glad we've moved past it – it sounds primitive, ridiculous."

"That is exactly what I have been taught," Mel says. "I was raised to see the mystics as fools at best and dangerous at worst. I agreed." She sighs wearily. "Yes, I agreed that it was all that you say – dangerous, primitive. Foolish. That's what I thought, until. . ." Mel leans her chair back to reach something off her desk – it's the notebook she's been carrying around with her. "Until it happened to me."

I open my mouth but I can't speak. Her tone is matter-of-fact, but there is something embarrassed, proud, nervous in her expression. She believes this is true.

She goes on. "It started the day Mayor Longsight was attacked. At night, I always have this notebook on my bedside table – when I have too many thoughts going around my head to sleep, I scribble them down and it eases my mind enough to let me rest. I had a lot on my mind that day.

"I wrote down what happened – that the mayor was attacked by a blank terrorist, that he had died. That the town was in a state of turmoil and grief. Then I put my notebook back on the nightstand and went to sleep." She leans forward. "But, when I woke up in the morning, the notebook was on my bed, open, and I'd filled pages with writing." She turns the pages and I see tightly written text, in a slanting hand – it goes on for pages.

There is a silence. Then I say, "You must have been unsettled and written it when you were only half awake. People do all kinds of things in their sleep. Mum used to fold clothes." I don't know if I'm explaining this away for Mel's benefit or my own, but I find the whole thing unnerving.

She nods. "Exactly what I told myself. I didn't even read it. I just shut the notebook, decided I'd had a strange dream. The mayor had just been stabbed – there was no time to dwell on it. But last night, it happened again."

"Coinciding with Mayor Longsight's latest stunt," I say slowly.

"And so I read it," she said quietly. "It's the same story, written out twice. Word for word identical." Mel's face is pale, and her eyes beg me to believe her. "I wouldn't make something like this up, Leora."

Mel has more to lose than to gain by telling me this. This is the kind of thing that could discredit her and cause people to doubt her skill and authority. It could make her a laughing stock. If anyone found out, then Mayor

Longsight might dismiss her to ensure her voice no longer carried weight in the life and teaching of Saintstone. It would be so much easier for her to keep this quiet. Why should she trust me?

"I believe you," I say and immediately something softens between us. We are in this together now, not mentor and student but allies. Mel leans forward and grasps my hand.

"Thank you." She comes to sit next to me, bringing the notebook with her. "I'm scared," she murmurs. "But this is a message – and I think that there is light here," she taps the notebook, "and hope too."

"What is the story about?" I ask.

"I hoped you would ask." She smiles shyly. "Would you let me read it to you?"

Chapter Sixteen

The Sisters

Neither of them could say what had made them come, but here they both were. Moriah and Belia – sisters united by blood and divided by ink – had not seen one another for many years. Belia's hair was salt-and-pepper grey and Moriah's rosebud lips were bracketed by lines.

At first each twin thought they had walked into a trap, a trick of the other's making. They circled the crumbling cottage, looking for danger, but all they found were thorns and spiders. Belia and Moriah met at the front door, the weathered entrance to the house where they had grown up, and, eyeing one another guardedly, they each placed a hand to the door and pushed. The swollen wood and rusting hinges groaned as they shifted and, for the first time in many decades, light shone into the cottage.

Belia built a fire and collected clean water from the old well. Moriah washed dust-encrusted cups and drew from her satchel a folded envelope of tea. As steam rose from the enamel kettle over the fire, the sisters sat and warmed their hands.

"We both left in a hurry." Belia broke their silence. The women looked around at the house: a museum of their former lives. "You for marriage and me for survival."

"You make me sound selfish," Moriah complained. "I fell in love. Father would have been glad to see me so happy."

"Our father fed on our misery. Your marriage was an escape after he left us with nothing but a curse." Belia's voice was gentle but her eyes were sad.

"A curse?" Moriah's lovely face creased into a frown.

"You never did believe in it, did you?" Belia tutted and poured the tea.

"I don't know what you're talking about, Beli. I remember Father's dying wish — but it was a blessing from him. That's why my skin is illustrated with my story — you can hardly call me cursed."

"Something is wrong with your memory, Mora. If our father had a wish it was a wish for nothing but sadness. His life was a failure and so he wanted the same cruel fate for us. That is why you are marked — surely you can't still believe that your inked skin is good? You may as well be naked for all the privacy your body provides you. It's obscene to live so blatantly; where is your pride?"

"This again." Moriah sighed. "Haven't enough years passed? Are you still so envious of my good fortune? Don't think I've forgotten the ways you attempted to hijack my happiness and position. Perhaps I can agree that you are cursed, but don't tar me with the same brush. I am a queen."

A crackle of fire, a scent of dust baking in the growing heat, a melodious slurp of tea, but the sisters were otherwise silent. Sun peeped in through the foggy window and left Belia sat in the shadow while Moriah was bathed in dawn light. Two sides, two shades, two sisters, once womb-close and now torn apart by their stories.

Belia went to the window and pulled down the half-hitched curtain, filling the small space with the light from outside. She turned and saw that there were no shadows now, no cold spots or hiding places. Sitting down once again she poured more tea and gazed thoughtfully at her sister.

"Moriah, tell me your story," Belia said softly. "Tell me how you remember life in this cottage back when we were young." Moriah was quiet for some time, staring into the fire.

"I remember Mother," Moriah began. "I remember her voice and how she would sing sweetly when it was time for us to sleep. I used to lie with one eye open and watch her and Father dance. They would try to scold me when I gave myself away by giggling when they bumped into the table, but they were laughing too, and they kissed me goodnight through smiles. But then she was gone. Father would still tuck us in at night, but there was no more singing. He told stories instead, do you remember? And as I grew older I would sing the songs our mother sang, and it made him smile. You were such a quiet child; I wondered whether you ever adjusted after Mother died. But when you began writing down Father's stories it gave me

hope – it felt as though we were a team. He would tell, I would sing, and you would write.

Then when he died you disappeared too; you spent days walking in the darkest corners of the wood. Father had wished for us to take our stories with us, but you seemed determined to avoid having any story to tell at all. And so, when the prince came by I was more than glad to go with him, for I knew you despised me – perhaps I reminded you of all we had lost. I thought that in leaving you I was giving you what you longed for: the chance to rewrite your life without me."

Moriah reached out and touched her sister's unmarked skin; she held her hand and looked into her dark eyes.

"I never meant for us to become enemies, Belia. I hoped you would join me, but you were obstinate: bent on destroying all the good things that came my way."

Belia squeezed her sister's hand and smiled sadly.

"I think I understand more now. I'm sorry I left you; I see now that it must have appeared that I hated you and wished to deny you happiness. I never wanted us to be enemies either, sister; but listen to my story, for I wonder if our father did."

Moriah sat back in her chair, ignoring its creaking joints.

"I remember our mother's songs too, Mora; and I remember when they stopped. However, this seems to be where the similarities in our stories end. I recall how Father would force you to sing, even when you said you were tired or told him that singing our mother's songs made you sad."

90

"He just wanted so desperately to be reminded of her – he . . . he didn't force me." Moriah's denial comes quickly, her voice high and sure.

"Moriah, you are a queen, but you do not rule over me. Please listen to my tale as I listened to yours."

Moriah's mouth opened, as if ready to admonish a servant, but she paused and nodded, gesturing for Belia to continue.

"I was no use to him. I didn't remind him of the past and I gave him no hope that I would be an asset in the future. He would often tell me that he rejoiced at your birth, Moriah, but that when it became apparent that there was another baby he burned with hatred. I had stolen space in his household, an uninvited visitor. He would whisper to me that I was a curse, a message from evil spirits, a terrible intruder on the life he had planned. He would hold my head and make me look at you and your beauty; he would make me listen to you and he would tell me that you, so like your mother, were his only child. Moriah, I wonder if you ever remember me speaking? Did you ever notice that I was silent? Our father forbade me to speak in the house: my only task beyond the chores he had me do was to write down his stories, word for word. He would take away my food if I got even one word wrong. I hated him and yet wished for his love. When he was dying I kept feeling a tickle in my chest as though I might laugh at any moment, for the only way I could live was if he died."

Belia sipped her tea and placed another log on the fire.

"But he wouldn't even give me that. He cursed us on his

deathbed and it is only because I broke the curse that I am here today."

Wiping tears from her cheeks, Moriah said, "I don't remember . . . I don't remember any of that. How can our stories be so different?"

"People would often say the same about you and me, Moriah: how can they be so different? But we were – we are – and yet we are still sisters."

"What do I believe then, if my story isn't true?" Moriah weeps.

"Why do you say that? Why do you say your story is no longer true?" Belia asked.

"Because it can't be true, not if he did all that to you."

Belia only sighed.

"Sister, I think this is where we have been battling all our lives: each of us with a story, each of us certain that our story is the only one that matters – the only real truth. I wish I had known how you saw our childhood – I had assumed that you hated me like our father did."

"I never saw it, Belia – I am so sorry. I was in my own world, I never thought to check what your world was like."

"I wonder if this is what Father wanted – to keep us separate from one another by meddling with our stories. Moriah, I don't think we need to fight about whose story is the truest; I don't think the existence of my story blots out the need for yours. I think that both stories together give us a new truth – a better, messier truth."

"I have been so lonely without you." Moriah held out her hands to her sister.

"I have found my missing piece." Belia entwined her fingers with Moriah's.

The story ends with a picture – a line drawing of two women: one inked, one blank, hands clasped, foreheads touching: faces close enough for a kiss.

Chapter Seventeen

There is a silence after Mel finishes talking. My heart is beating fast. This story, my dreams, the mark that Mel showed me, inked on ancient skin – and the mark appearing on my own stomach. This can't be a coincidence.

I drop to my knees before her and, quickly, before I can think better of it, I lift my shirt.

Her breath catches. She covers her mouth with her hand. With shaking fingers, she reaches her free hand towards me and touches the mark. At first, she is gentle and tentative and then her touch is firm: wiping at the lines to check, to make sure this is not some trick.

Minutes pass and at last, Mel lifts her face and looks into my eyes. I don't know whether I want to laugh or cry. The unbearable energy shooting around my body mixes fear with excitement. This is *something*; and time will tell whether it is something good or bad.

"I need some air." Mel fairly staggers to where her shawl is hung. "Come with me."

We walk out into the town square, warm sun stroking our bare arms and kissing our cheeks. Mel is used to attracting attention, especially when she is seen without guards or on official business. But I'm certain that my presence is amplifying the stares. The grass in the centre of the town square is intersected with footpaths, all meeting at the statue of Saint. The patches of green are muddied and worn from the crowd who stood here watching Mayor Longsight be marked yesterday. The statue itself has dust and grime clinging to it – an extra layer on Saint's skinless form. He has never been so neglected; but then, there is a new saviour now.

We are given a wide berth by the people who pass by. I'm not sure whether they are awed by Mel or horrified by me, but it works in our favour. We sit undisturbed on a bench and watch the pigeons while we talk together, processing all that we have found.

"Your story," I begin, "do you think it's true – an actual account of what happened for the sisters, or do you think it's a myth – a tale with a message for us to consider?"

"Interesting that you put those two in opposition. Can't something be both true and mythical? For me, I think it confirms our suspicions that the skin I showed you tells of a time when the sisters reunited. So, in that sense, it is a true tale – based on reality. But there's always more to a story than simply acting as a record. It is meant to sit with us and mature until it becomes something powerful."

I understand what she means. "Either way, I don't think it's chance that those stories came to you when they did," I say. "Mayor Longsight claims to have been restored from the dead – this voice appears. He claims to take on the sins of others – again, this voice. It's as though ... as though it wants you to hear a different story."

She nods sombrely. "I'm afraid, Leora," she says quietly. "My stories have always been the ones the people expected – the tales they already knew. I have acted, I thought, in their best interests when I used my voice to support our leaders. But this story – this different ending for the sisters – I would be a lone voice, and no one would want to hear me. Because this story goes against everything we hold dear: the people love their enmity with the blanks; it gives them something to believe in, unites them. They would not know what to do with a message of peace." She chews her lip. "Mayor Longsight is offering them something extraordinary – the chance to purge sin without suffering. That's all they want to hear right now."

I shift my foot to ward off a pigeon that has come too close and it hops away in a flurry of feathers. Uncomfortable with the thoughts in my head, I say them out loud. One of us has to.

"But he's alive. Longsight died and now he's alive. I've seen the wound – it's like a fresh injury and a healed scar all at once. And the people watched him die – they paraded around his body to pay respects. So, if that happened, then why aren't the ancestors telling you *that* story? Why aren't they vindicating it?" I rub my forehead. "There are no teachings which indicate that such a thing is possible. The ancestors speak to a storyteller for the first time in centuries, and they do not tell of this amazing resurrection, but of the sisters. Why?"

She looks troubled. "He was dead, Leora. I attended when they let the townspeople come to see his body. For one hour a day they were allowed into the government building and trooped past, his still form on a high platform. I remember thinking he was like the statue of Saint: cold and lifted up for us to remember. And yet, within days he walked with us, like a ghost. I don't know how it happened, but I can't deny it."

I shake my head stubbornly. "No. The ancestors could have told that story, but instead they spoke of a message left in the preserved skin and my mark appears. That is the story that is real. Mel, I don't know how it happened, but Longsight tricked us."

She shakes her head, but I know she thinks the same. We just don't know how he did it.

"What do we do?" she says helplessly. "I am the

storyteller and I have a story... I should tell it to my people. It is my duty."

I look at her, at the anguish on her face. "I don't think you should yet," I say. "I think we wait. The ancestors are trying to tell you something and they've already shown that they are willing to repeat themselves until they get your attention. I don't think they will leave you now." I squeeze her arm. "Let's be patient. We watch."

Chapter Eighteen

Be patient.

Such an easy thing to say, but I had forgotten that as soon as you have to be patient, time slows down.

Mel gives me freedom to wander, as long as I don't go outdoors. This means I have the run of the museum and, once I've remembered the winding route of the underground access, I can access the jail too.

I visit Obel often. I have to sit on the floor in the walkway in order to speak to him. He smiles when he sees me. He is clean, well fed and no beatings have marred his painted ink.

"They still have plans for you, then," I say one day.

"Looks like it." He shrugs. "Not that they tell me anything."

A husky voice comes from behind me.

"Ah, they tell you enough, Obel." It's Connor. His dark skin has no shine and his eyes are glassy, but there is playfulness and cunning in his voice.

I turn to Obel and frown. "Do you know more than you're telling me?" He sighs and shakes his head.

"They tell me I am to mark the mayor, they tell me it will win me some comfort. I'm instructed what mark to make and I make it. There's nothing more to tell."

"Come, Obel, I know you're locked up but don't let it rot your brain," Connor says, his tone kind beneath his chiding words. "You're a blank who lived among us for years: deceived an entire town. If Longsight told the people that, the good citizens of Saintstone would be baying for your blood. And yet . . . Longsight lets you live and he keeps your secret. Why? Come on, inker, think about it."

Obel gives him a faint smile. I look at Connor. His ink is beautiful beneath the dirt. His marks are reminiscent of harvest festivals; I can see that his parents were farmers. His skin celebrates the hard work of labouring finally celebrated with a glut of fruit and grain and vegetables. A tattoo of a corn dolly swirls into a memory of when Connor would come home from the flayers, kiss his wife and baby son – Oscar – and his heart would feel like it was fit to burst from all the love and joy and plenty they enjoyed. Ink that shows a wide sunset above a reaped field tells me of the emptiness when his wife died – of how it seemed like all their blessings had wasted away. I've never seen this bit of Oscar's life and I wonder now at how hard it must have been to always be trying to fill the space left by his mother.

"All right, genius," Obel says softly. "Tell us why you think I'm here."

He smiles. "Glad you asked." He crouches on his haunches, making himself more comfortable. "The mayor could use any inker – there are plenty of the government inkers who usually do the official marks that he could choose. But he's got *you*, Obel. And that's because he can use you. You have a secret. He can keep you close. Why? Because he's planning something."

Obel chews his lip. "We should speak to Karl," he murmurs.

"Karl?" I ask, and Obel hushes me.

"Karl Novak. He's one of us, isn't he?" Connor grins, his voice barely audible. "He's joined the crows."

Before I can register my surprise a guard interrupts us. Our time is up and I'm asked to leave, a strong hand on my back pressing me away from Obel. I turn my head and he's watching me leave. Connor Drew has given us both plenty to think about.

Fingers and fire. Together they make pictures on the wall – shadows that dance and play. Stories breed in the shade.

From the shadows rises a man and the fire spits out two words: *saviour* and *spy*.

The outline of the man splits in two and these identical figures enact a different story. One shows a man who has pity on his enemies; he goes to them and shares all that he has.

The other man also visits his enemy, but this man becomes a fox that wriggles its way through the community.

The first man is broken by his enemy – his skin is shed and he drags it like spoils of the hunt.

The second man breaks away, taking his enemy's children with him.

I want to still those fingers, put out the fire – I don't want to see any more. But a new figure rises and the flames breathe the word: *hero*.

I reach out to touch this person made from shadows, but when my fingers get close the shadow fades into smoke. The fire is out and I am in darkness. The puppeteer's fingers trace their way up my spine and I shiver.

Chapter Nineteen

I wake from my dream, my teeth chattering. I go for a walk to clear my head and see Jack Minnow. He still visits the hall of remembrance every night. As I watch him in the moonlight, he looks up at the window where I stand, and our eyes meet. He smiles. I am waiting, biding my time. I want to know more first – who is Davey Minnow and why risk so much to remember him?

The days pass, and Mel has no more new tales written in her notebook. It is irking her, keeping her story inside. After a week, she snaps.

"This is ridiculous." Mel throws down her pen and lets her chair scrape as she stands. "I'm the storyteller; I have authority of my own. We're going to see him. I'm going to tell Longsight my new story."

"No, Mel—" But she is gone, walking fast. I run to keep up with her, and am almost dizzied as we turn corner after corner, finally finding ourselves outside Mayor Longsight's study. I catch her arm.

"Please don't do this," I whisper. "We need more time..."

But Mel holds her hand up for silence. And that's when I realize: the door is ajar, and we hear familiar voices. We lean closer to the door and listen.

"Tell me again," Mayor Longsight is saying. "Tell me how it happened."

There is a pause and then Jack Minnow speaks, his voice carrying. "You were pronounced dead. Carried into the mourning room, and we gathered about you for three days. And then it was time for your final journey. We prepared you. And then I heard it – a gasp. The faintest sound.

"I cleared the room; it was just you and me. I hardly dared believe it, but it was so. You were breathing. Your prediction was true, and my delight burned in me. When you spoke first, I knew I had to record your words." I hear the shunt of a drawer opening and the crackle of paper. "It's all there – you've read it many times. A message from the grave, sir."

"It's all so hard to remember." The mayor sounds weary. There is a period of silence which seems to stretch for ever. "But it happened, just like you said. It must have done."

"I trust you, Mayor Longsight," Minnow says. "You must learn to trust yourself. This new teaching was given

106

to you by our ancestors. There can be no doubt of this course."

"But the blanks..." Mayor Longsight says. "The people want their destruction: they want victory."

"And victory they will get: victory of a different sort. Be strong."

There is a pause and when Longsight speaks again he sounds cold. "I *am* strong, Minnow. I know my mind – I am simply concerned for the people."

"Understood." Jack Minnow clears his throat.

Mel catches my arm. She leads me down the corridor, back to her rooms, and even when the door is shut behind us and we are safe we do not speak of what we've heard.

Instead, we fold up the memory of that conversation. We tuck it away for another time. One day it will make sense.

I am just afraid that by the time that happens, it will be too late.

Chapter Twenty

Exactly one week after Mayor Longsight was marked in the place of a guilty citizen, the people are once again called to gather in the square, and again, I am made to attend. We walk together, me, Mel and Obel – guards to our left and right, Karl Novak leading us. He doesn't look my way this time.

Just before we reach the door that takes us to the back of the stage, Jack Minnow seizes my elbow, sending pain flashing up and down my arm.

"Just in case you were planning on doing something foolish, I thought I'd remind you not to. You haven't forgotten your little blank friend, have you?" he growls. "Do as you're told, Flint. That is all." And with one last dig of his fingernails, he lets me go.

I stand at the side of the stage, waiting for the next show. Minnow's warning has made me more nervous.

The crowd are more eager than ever – the mayor's act of kindness towards the prisoner Phillip Knowles has thrilled them. Maybe they are hoping that they will be next.

He leaves them waiting, poised in the wings. The day is hot and close, the kind of sky that makes flies dozy and people aggressive. A chant goes up, the people calling his name like a magic rite. And when I think they might melt or explode or die with the heat, the energy, the thrall of it all, there is a squeal of feedback and the crowd is silent.

It takes only one step on to the stage for the whoops to restart, and Longsight wallows in their adulation. He is wearing a robe and the silken fabric sways against his arms as he holds his hands out either side of him. He basks in the glow of their screamed approval. He has never been so loved as this; and with love comes power.

"You are good to me," Longsight begins. "I know that you have made sacrifices to be here today – you have closed your shops and market stalls, switched off your machines, cancelled meetings. Even the schools have let out their students." There is an enthusiastic cheer at this – the pupils are in a large group near the front. The adults around them smile indulgently – give them their exuberance, let them feel the excitement of a disrupted school day. This doesn't happen every day.

"I assure you that I don't call these gatherings lightly. No, I brought you here to be my witnesses – to share in something truly wonderful. For today, this very morning, a miracle has happened. Yes, another! We will be used to miracles before long." His mouth twists into a knowing smile. *But miracles aren't meant to happen every day*, I think. *That's the whole point.*

He points to the crowd, picking out a person near the front whose brown hair and bright eyes shine as she looks up at her leader. "You," he says, "come up to the stage."

She raises her eyebrows and points to her chest, questioning, *Me? Really?* Longsight nods. "And you. . ." He points to another person and another and another. There is an excited bustle as guards help the blushing, smiling people on to the stage. They stand a few metres away from the mayor, looking at each other in surprised wonder, not ready to believe their luck at being chosen. But chosen for what? Jack Minnow steps up to the stage too – acting as a bodyguard or an assistant. He stands close to the mayor, face impassive.

"You watched, just a week ago, as I was inked," the mayor continues. "You saw it happen – you knew I went willingly under the needle so that our friend Philip did not have to." He knows how to whip the crowd into an excited rabble and they respond exactly as he will have planned: applause, stamps and whoops of praise.

Mayor Longsight holds up his right hand, to hush them. "I deserve none of your acclaim," he says solemnly. "I was simply obeying a command. Following my calling.

My ancestors told me what to do while I ate at Death's table."

I can feel my cynicism pressing on my shoulders. I look across at Mel, who stands next to me. For the briefest moment, scepticism is written on her face too.

We must be careful.

"When I woke this morning, it was from the most beautiful dream," the mayor tells us. "A dream where I found a hidden waterfall – I can still hear it if I close my eyes – the roar and rush of it. In my dream, I removed my robes." As he speaks, he unties the belt on his robe. "And I stepped forward, the water freezing on my bare feet. I did not stop – I did not fear the cold." He tugs at the tie and his robe falls open, shrugs it off his shoulders so it rests in the crook of his elbows – we can see his chest, his breath strong and steady. He takes a step forward. "In my dream I walked into the beating flood." His robe drops to the ground. "And the water washed away my sin." He moves to the front of the stage – no microphone needed now, for his body says it all.

The mark that Obel made on Mayor Longsight's arm is gone.

The mayor walks the width of the stage, letting the crowd see – his left arm is bare and clean. Longsight moves to show the four witnesses who stand on the stage, each looking stunned and as though they want to cower, but Longsight makes them each examine his arm. They look, they are even allowed to touch. At this, the memory of being in Mayor Longsight's study and running my fingers over his scar shudders through me. I could not deny that miracle and I cannot deny this one either.

He is at the side of the stage near to where I am standing – close enough for me to see. There is no mark, no evidence of a tattoo that has been tampered with – no evidence of a wound at all. Just clear, brown skin. It is as though his body absorbed the ink and took it away.

I look for Obel. He must know the answer to this riddle, I think. But I can't see him anywhere. And then, just as the tension feels like it will snap our necks, a rumble of thunder drowns out the shouts. Mayor Longsight stands on the stage, face raised to the sky and arms outstretched. As if answering his call, the rain begins – fat drops that hammer so heavily it is as though a tap was switched on. As though a waterfall opened above us. And Mayor Longsight stands perfect beneath the stream. His sin washed away, like mud from weary feet.

Jack Minnow looks down from the stage and gestures to Karl, who is standing guard next to me. Karl pushes me towards the stage. I turn to Mel and her face shows fear. Minnow looks at me with twisted pleasure, as though he is watching a hunted creature walk right into his trap. Now I understand why he warned me. I am to play a part in today's performance.

I am left standing on the steps up to the stage, Karl gripping tightly on to my shoulder. Jack Minnow steps to the front of the watery stage where Mayor Longsight still glories in the praises of his people. Moving close to the microphone, Minnow begins to speak.

"We know that in our hearts, each of us now long for this – we can only dream that we would be one of the lucky ones that our great Mayor Longsight would take on ink for. But today, we will mark our mayor with the most heinous sins. You will see the full extent of his power and his grace as he takes on the crimes of one of our most depraved citizens."

That is me, I think dully. I am shoved forward by the guards. And then Karl murmurs something in my ear. It sounds like, "Don't be afraid." I freeze, but when I look at him his expression is impassive.

"Come, Leora," says Minnow. He turns to me and his face is cruel. "Come."

I take a step forward, and then another.

There is movement in the crowd. At first I think it is because they see me, but then I realize it is coming from the back. Like a trickle that becomes a flood, the murmurs from the back of the crowd become screams as someone – one small messenger, an ordinary citizen of Saintstone – pushes their way through the throng. I think I recognize her as the woman who runs a small farm on the outskirts of town – she has wild, curling grey hair and a weather-beaten face. With Minnow focused on the mayor and the guards taken by surprise, in mere seconds the woman pushes past me and is on the stage standing at the microphone.

"They've taken them!" she screams, tears streaming down her face faster than the rain. "They've taken them. My books!"

In the shocked silence that follows, it is Mel who goes to her.

She holds her by her shoulders – firmly but kindly. The woman turns, her face a blank page of grief, and she tumbles into Mel's open arms. The crowd are silent now. There is just the sound of the rain and the woman's shuddering sobs. I see her mouth move as she speaks. At last, Mel's arms drop and like a mechanical doll she walks to the microphone. She swallows before she speaks.

"There has been a break-in." Mel is so used to addressing a crowd, often she has no need of amplification for her training has given her voice reach and resonance. But today she is flat, and her voice sounds as though it's being squeezed through a small space. "A break-in at Shona Collier's farm. They left everything untouched except for. . ." Mel holds out her hand to the weeping woman, who takes it gratefully. "Except for . . . the skin books."

"They've taken my family!" The woman howls, and her words stab every chest.

When I was a child there was a fire at the Coopers' house on our street. The shouts went up and the fire brigade was called, but it felt like an age before they arrived. I stood next to Mum, with bare feet and my nightie, feeling the heat that came off the blazing house.

My dad held Mr Cooper back, kept having to fight to keep hold of him because he was frantic and repeating the same thing over and over:

"They're still in there – I have to save them," he said, while his wife stood screaming, "My children!"

Dad had shaken him then, stared into his eyes and shouted over the roar.

"They're not there, Jonathan," he yelled. "They are not there – they're already gone."

His words were heresy. But now I see that he was saving a life, not squandering two. Because Mr Cooper's children had both died when they were babies. It was their skin books he wanted to save.

Without a skin book there is no soul. When I allowed Dad's book to be burned – believing at the time that it really was his – I was destroying his very soul. This is why we keep the books close to us. They are how we live on after death. They are our guarantee of eternity. I never came across the crime of stealing a skin book from another person's home. Even the most depraved heart would draw back. It is beyond taboo.

We all look to Longsight, to our great leader, but he is staring, open-mouthed, shocked. He seems diminished somehow. His performance today has not gone to plan. Instead, it is Jack Minnow who steps to the mic, and he and Mel stand tall together.

"Go back to your homes," he calls. "Do not panic. We will find the answers and we will not rest until the evildoer has been brought to justice. This I swear to you."

There are no cheers now; the people stumble away, casting fearful glances backwards. You can tell people not to panic, but it only makes the fear greater. Because in our town someone has committed the unforgivable.

And Mayor Longsight? He watches his worshippers wash away in the rain. Their adoration has run through his fingers, their awe has turned to dread. His face is all fury – his spotlight was stolen, and to him, that is another unforgiveable act.

Chapter Twenty-one

Back in Mel's study, I pace. It is the blanks, it must be. Only they would commit this sacrilege, this terrible thing. And only one person will be blamed for bringing them here – me. I'm surprised a lynch mob isn't outside already, baying for my blood.

Mel bursts in, breathless and flushed.

"Start packing," she tells me, flinging a bag at me.

"I don't have anything to pack." I say, bewildered. "I have nothing, remember? Anyway, where do you think we're going?"

"Featherstone, of course," she says, matter-of-factly. She glances at me, shoving her notebook into her bag. "They took the books, didn't they? Or do you have other ideas?"

"No," I admit. I take the armful of clothes Mel hands me and stuff them into a bag. "No one else would steal a skin book. The crime has Sana written all over it."

"Agreed." Mel hands me a bar of soap.

"What do you think going to Featherstone will achieve?" I ask curiously.

"Well," she says, wrapping a shawl around herself. "I think we need to go there in the capacity of peacemakers." She smiles at my surprised face. "Longsight's new teachings, as extraordinary as they are, have done one thing. Distracted the people from the blanks. This could actually be a chance for peace, if Sana doesn't blow it." She chews her lip. "We have to take it, Leora. The prophecy wants us to."

I want to say that I don't think Sana will be so easily convinced into peace, but I know we have to try. We must attempt to fix the void between the blanks and marked – maybe this is what the story of the sisters was telling us to do.

But how does this fit in with Longsight, and his strange new powers?

"Mel," I say, "do you really think he came back from the dead? Do you think his marks vanished? *Was* it a miracle?"

She is suddenly still and now I see it, the thing that has been driving her. Fear.

"The mark was real," Mel admits quietly. "Obel inked him – we saw the needle push into his skin – and now the line is gone. A miracle? I don't know, but I do know that whatever Longsight and Minnow are planning, whether

120

it is miraculous or not, it will only mean more power for them and less freedom for the people. Whatever he says, however generous he might appear, the mayor will always put his own needs first."

I nod, and continue packing. Within moments we are ready.

"Won't they notice?" I ask tentatively. "We can't just leave, can we?"

"Of course we can," she says, sounding braver than she must feel. "I strutted around the government building making a nuisance of myself, demanding extra measures in these extreme times. Eventually, I declared that I would travel to Riverton with my charge (that's you, Leora) to call for their wisdom and support. It buys us time and it gives us reason to leave Saintstone unobstructed. We have even been given horses." She grins. "The mayor can't wait for us to leave. Now. You do remember how to get to Featherstone, don't you?"

Chapter Twenty-two

The horses are sure-footed, but there are times where I take us down a wrong path and we have to turn back. It was quicker when I was riding with Sana because, of course, she knew the forest perfectly. Although I remember the route, I still need to check for the right landmarks, and it's becoming noticeably darker with unnerving speed.

"They will already know we're coming," I tell Mel. "The blanks. They watch the routes from Saintstone."

She shrugs. "I'm counting on it."

"If you're counting on them being pleased to see me, well … they won't be rolling out a great welcome, Mel. I left under a cloud, and Sana will have made sure to muddy my name since I've been gone." I shiver, remembering my last few days in Featherstone. Dragging Gull from the water under the forbidding gaze of the community. That terrible discovery, that Sana had been starving and infecting her own people, to agitate for war with the marked. That bloodstained knife. The horror of

Longsight's death. Riding away from Oscar, every step feeling like my heart was being wrenched out of my chest. Leaving behind Tanya and Solomon and Fenn, all good people, to pick up the pieces.

"You still care for them, though." Mel reaches up and brushes a branch with her hand as she passes underneath.

"I do," I say fiercely. "I care that they're being mistreated by Sana and they don't seem to realize it. She has been keeping resources from the people: food, medicine, clothes. The way she sees it, the hungrier the people are, the more angry they will be with Saintstone. She needs their anger. She is desperate to wage war."

"I wonder why," Mel says thoughtfully. "It's not a war they could easily win. Does she *want* to win – or does she want to fight?"

"She's been let down by people she loved and trusted." I think of how she talked about my birth mum, her best friend, Miranda, falling in love with Dad and how, to her, it was the worst possible betrayal.

"You've been let down too, Leora, and yet you're not like Sana. I've seen you angry, true – but I've never seen that anger turn to hate." She smiles briefly. "Well, maybe just once."

I frown, dreading what she might say next. Mel slows her horse and we ride side by side.

"You were raised to hate the blanks. We all were.

All of us in Saintstone are taught from an early age that these are evil beings who are desperate to steal our souls. So little wonder that you hated your father when you heard that he had married a blank. You hated him all the more when you realized you were that blank woman's daughter and he had kept all this from you. It was fear and anger and self-loathing that led you to hate him enough to see his book burned."

I swallow, remembering that day, the hatred that coursed through me bittersweet as wine.

"But that hate left you quickly," Mel goes on. "And you have since acted to resist it. Sana is different. We can develop our anger into hate by feeding it with fear and ignorance, blame and bitterness. But eventually, the hate devours us."

We ride in silence for a while and the fragrances of the forest rise up to greet us. Everything is just a breath away from full bloom, the buds and leaves fit to burst with life. The ground beneath the horses' hooves gives up a herbal scent of rain and ritual, and I think of Gull taking me through the forest, walking barefoot and smiling at her surroundings as though they were her only friend.

"Tell me more," Mel says after a while. "Was Sana really the one who killed Longsight?"

"She was the one who stabbed him, yes." I remember that night. The night that Gull painted her skin with a paste of ash that burned her, desperate for a mark of her own, Oscar holding her arm under running water. Fenn telling us that we had to leave. And then the final piece of the puzzle falling into place. The box with Sana's black clothing and red knife.

She confessed to us that very night – as though admitting to a ruse. She gloried in it – she knew the people's hunger made them desperate for something to fill them, and that something, she had decided, was her – her as their leader, her as warmonger, her as the one person who could bring them victory. The people thought she meant all this to bring peace – when really all she wanted was the fight.

I dread to imagine what kind of a town I am returning to, what will be left of the people I care so much for. But Mel knows so little of Featherstone and its community – how can I prepare her for what she is about to find? A whole world of opposite.

"When I travelled through the forest with Sana the first time, she spoke of regular meetings with envoys from Saintstone – the crows," I tell Mel. I look at her cautiously. She must know the crows exist, but I have never talked about them with her. "She was just a kid, but she would be taken along sometimes. They would gather here and hand over resources: food and medical items and clothing. But I think it was a meeting of friends too; they would share food and messages and stories." This makes Mel sit straighter.

"What else do you know of the crows?" Mel asks. Her voice is neutral and I glance at her again.

"Not as much as I would like," I admit. "I know Obel, Oscar and Connor were – *are* – part of the group, and they felt the blanks were unfairly treated and would bring them supplies and news. And I think my dad was too, or at least he supported them. Agreed with what they were doing. But I don't know how it works or who the rest of them are."

I look to her for more, but she is quiet. Mel is thoughtful for much of our time riding – gazing around her at new sights, amazed at the way the light plays through the leaves creating shadows and glimmers that dance together.

Chapter Twenty-three

"We just cross the river here," I say, nodding ahead. "You're sure about this?"

Mel nods and we lead our horses over the bridge. I remember a story Dad used to tell about goats *trip-trapping* over a bridge and a troll threating to eat them. I didn't like that one – it scared me. Made me wonder what else was under bridges and beds waiting to leap out.

We still have a way to go before we reach Featherstone, but we're on their land now. I turn at every sound and try not to be lulled by the familiar giggle of the river water.

It's a surprise, then, when it's not an ambush that stops us, but a friend. A friend with hands up and a smile on his face a mile wide.

Oscar.

"Whoa!" he says in a deep lullaby voice, and the horses slow, not fazed by his appearance. He knows exactly how to behave. He always does. He comes near and rests his hand palm-flat between my horse's eyes. He whispers to him and rubs his neck. Oh, I wish I was a horse. Oscar looks up at me and I blush extravagantly. "Fancy seeing you here." His grin pulls me in and I let myself go.

I feel woozy as Mel and I walk, leading the horses, following Oscar, who has told us to save conversation for later. I don't know whether the giddiness comes from being used to the rock and sway of being in the saddle or just the spinning feeling of seeing Oscar and the relief that he is OK. He's leading us away from the path I would normally take. Oscar said we needed to be careful and quiet and to take a different route. He looks back at me now and then, each time with that smile that dazzles me more than a sunset.

We emerge into a clearing made by a fallen tree. The remaining foliage has grown gingerly up and outwards, and as the light pours down, the fur of moss and the pale scales of lichen make the low, twisting branches look like creatures. In the clearing is a tent and a fire, besides which sit Tanya and Solomon. They look at us with wide eyes as we enter their dwelling. There is a pause, and then they stand up and, to my overwhelming relief, Tanya pulls me to her in a crushing hug.

"I have so much to tell you," I whisper into her shoulder. "Gull is fine, she's safe." *Please let this be true.* "But I couldn't bring her with me."

She hushes me.

"You can tell me everything, Leora."

The smell of woodsmoke and Tanya's hair makes me feel like I'm coming home. To one of my homes, at least.

Oscar ties the horses up and Mel looks at us as though she is ready to back away and run – her fingers clasp, knuckles white, and her breath is quick. I suppose I thought she would be regal even here, that she would walk into Featherstone, head up, back so straight, and remove her cloak in a sweeping flow, revealing her full colours. But she is shrunken in the forest; she looks at the blank skin of Tanya and Solomon and I see her swallow back years of ingrained fear and disgust.

It's Tanya who moves.

"You are welcome." She holds out both hands to Mel. "I am Tanya, this is Solomon – and Oscar, obviously, you know. Leora is a daughter to us. Seeing Leora return is wonderful; seeing her return with a friend is even better."

Tanya's kindness is a lasting thing – like the north star or the frost in winter, you can rely on it to be there. A lump grows in my throat and I duck my head, thinking of her children, in Saintstone. One in a cell and the other . . . I don't know where. But safe, Longsight told me she would be safe.

Mel kneels on the floor before Tanya. She takes Tanya's hands, dips her head and says, "My name is Mel. I'm here as a friend. Thank you for your welcome." Only I can tell what effort it costs her. I see the White Witch on the storyteller's skin and imagine her cursing Mel for her treachery.

"We don't have much," Solomon says, to Mel and to me, and he gestures at the scraps of blankets and rolled bedding that they are using to sit on around the fire. "But what we have we share. Come, sit down. You must be thirsty?"

Solomon boils water over the fire and brings us a kind of tea made with yellow leaves. Although it's bitter, it is invigorating. Mel sips at hers cautiously. Mel: always given the best of everything when it comes to food and drink. I don't suppose she's ever had to force something down to be polite or simply to survive.

A silence covers us and a minute of calm passes, but beneath it, under the surface, the question floats. Where is Gull?

"Gull is safe," I blurt out again, and then I realize that is all I *can* say.

"Why is she not with you?" Tanya's chin quivers. "Doesn't she want to see us?" She grips my hand desperately and I wish I had more to tell her, better answers at least.

"Longsight is alive," I say and I see their eyes widen in shock. "And I was captured the minute I got back. Gull was taken in." I will myself to be brave – to be truthful.

It's the least the Whitworths deserve. "Tanya, I am so sorry – I don't know where Gull is, but I have been told she is safe." Safe as long as I'm not found out. As long as no one knows I came to Featherstone. Safe . . . if I can trust a word Jack Minnow says.

Tanya's hand goes to her chest and her eyes close. She nods, as though she knows this story – as though she was just waiting for me to say it.

There is barely any food, but the Whitworths share with us a broth and we offer them all our goods. They marvel at the sight of cheese and Tanya laughs when she picks up the bread and says she might use it as a bed tonight, it is so soft. Apparently, on their first day here, Oscar tried to catch fish.

"I don't believe there are any in that river." He scowls when Solomon laughs at him.

"Not now that you scared them off." Solomon dodges a nudge from Oscar.

"Why are you here?" I ask. "Why aren't you home – in Featherstone with the others?"

The smile drops from Solomon's face. "Things have changed quickly for us too."

A sudden yelp of pain interrupts us. In the dying light, Mel is gathering firewood and she's already got a splinter. Tanya removes it and gives Mel a poultice to rub into the wound. "It wouldn't do to get an infection out here."

"It's just a tiny cut! It's hardly going to kill me," Mel exclaims.

"No, but blood poisoning could. We don't have the medical resources that you have. It is not worth risking."

Mel goes quiet as she holds the mulched-up leaf to her palm.

"How have you kept going out here?" she asks.

"Out here in the woods, or out here in Featherstone?" Tanya asks with a smile and a raised eyebrow.

"Both. I had never imagined it like this." She throws the herb on the fire and carries on collecting wood and twigs. "Actually, I had never imagined it at all. I refused to – what was the point of thinking about how you live, when all I really cared about was that you *didn't*?"

A kind of gasped silence leaves a vacuum between us – it is as though time has taken a breath. The quiet breaks with a twig under Mel's foot. "I was so blind. I still have so much to see." She lays her sticks in a neat pile at Tanya's feet, like an offering. "I hope you will show me."

Solomon speaks. "We have some help – a few in Featherstone care about us still. As for Featherstone – the crows bring them food, just like always. But there's less – the crows are having to be more circumspect. There are those in Saintstone who would have them destroyed."

"How do you know all this?" I ask. "Is Fenn still in Featherstone?"

Solomon nods proudly. "In many ways staying in Featherstone was riskier than leaving, but he did it. Once Oscar told us what Sana had been doing to the people – and had done to Longsight – we challenged her in front of the rest of the community. Our questioning was useless; she has them so convinced."

"She has them *terrified*," Tanya adds and Solomon nods.

"There was no choice for the three of us – Sana has banished us. She has made the people believe their hunger is our fault for being unfaithful. Fenn convinced Sana that he supported her in spite of all he'd seen that night you left with Gull. He let her believe that her actions made him want to follow her even more devotedly. Justus vouched for him."

Tanya gives Solomon's hand a squeeze. "Fenn's trying to help those we left – the innocent, ordinary people of Featherstone," she tells me. "Sana's still doing it, Leora – she's still keeping them in the dark, keeping them hungry and desperate." Clever, cruel Sana. "And it's working."

"Working how?" I ask, dread in my voice.

"Do you remember what it was like, Leora? To be so hungry? The hopeless hunger that you know won't recede, because you know that even if you eat something that day it won't be enough – it won't fill or satisfy."

"I remember it," I say quietly. And yet, I almost don't – it's strange how quickly I have forgotten. But I remember the fear. The idea that I might feel hunger like that again if I stay here leaves a terror in my bones that almost makes me run.

"How did you feel about Saintstone when you were hungry, Leora?" Tanya said softly. "What did you think when you knew their bellies were full while you ate mouldy bread?"

"I hated them," I whisper. And there is no lie there – I never felt more at home than when we were hungry together. More united in hatred. "I wanted to hurt them like they were hurting us." There is sad recognition in Oscar's face.

"They blame us," Tanya says, a little quietly. "According to the teaching, Gull was meant to stay beneath the water on her birth day ritual." I close my eyes and remember the cold of the dawn and the ice of water and the horror of Gull's limp body. "The verdict had been cast – she was meant to pay for her sins, for the sins of the people, by staying under. A sacrifice."

I swallow. It was me who dragged Gull out of the water that day. I did this. As if reading my mind, Tana lays a sudden hand on my arm. "And I will always be grateful to you for saving her – we will always be in your debt. But faith and tradition are powerful masters, Leora, as you know. Sana tells the people that their poverty, the land's exhaustion, their hunger and sickness, is not just the fault of the marked; it is also judgement upon them for their faithlessness. Because Gull did not pay the price, the land must pay instead. They are told every day that they live under a curse. The community have never been so devout – so watchful and wary of sin in their midst."

I think of Mayor Longsight and the way his acts of wonder have fostered new faith and belief.

"People want hope," I say. My voice sounds very small in the stillness.

"We all do," says Tanya. "But false hope is no hope at all."

Chapter Twenty-four

We eat bread and foraged salad leaves as darkness falls. Summer is not far off and the nights are shorter. But still, it is cold. After we finish, Tanya takes Mel off to wash, and Solomon prepares our sleeping area, leaving Oscar and me alone by the fire.

"Isn't it risky, having this fire?" I ask him.

"We need it. Besides, the people of Featherstone know where we are." I raise my eyebrows in surprise. "They wanted us gone from the settlement and they didn't really care where we went, as long as we're not with them. If they wanted to attack us, they've had time."

I lower my voice. "Why don't you come back? You have a home in Saintstone – you have the crows. You would be safe."

He is silent for a moment and then he looks at me. My heart races when he reaches out to hold my hand.

"I have a home here." Oscar's jaw tightens. "This is where I need to be – where I *choose* to be. They need help. I can't just leave."

His words hurt. I want him to say he is desperate to be wherever I am; foolishly, I want to matter more to him than anyone else – even the hungry people of Featherstone.

He brushes his thumb on my palm and my whole body feels like the fire.

"All my life Dad has raised me to think of the blanks first," Oscar says quietly. "Being part of the crows was, *is*, everything to him – especially after Mum died – and by joining the group myself I knew I would at least be linked to the thing he cared about most. He cares about destroying Longsight and uniting blank and marked, and that's it."

"Your father cares about *you*," I tell him. "I've seen him, read his marks – he's in the jail with Obel, he's in good spirits. You are the most important thing to him, not the crows."

Oscar forces a smile. "And he cares, does he? So how often did he ask about me, Leora? Did he mention my name?"

I pause and think back. I realize all the talk was about Obel and Mayor Longsight's plans. Oscar sees the expression on my face and nods.

"It was. . . He was trying to help Obel," I say uselessly. Oscar just shakes his head.

"It's OK, I'm used to it." He shrugs. "It's how it's always been."

I take his other hand in mine and make him look at me.

"You are wanted," I say. "Your father wants you, and I..." I tail off, feeling shaky and lost under his calm gaze.

"And you?" His voice is low and close.

"I assume everyone sees what I see ... and everyone feels how I feel." My head swims and my ears ring and I am only tethered by his hands holding on to mine.

"And how do you feel, Leora?" Oscar's eyes are searchlights, reading my face – I feel like he could read my mind too.

"I—"

"Our beds are all ready." Mel comes back towards the fire. I'm sure she sees Oscar and I drop hands and shift apart, but she makes no comment. I'm not sure whether I am glad or cross that we were interrupted, but when I look at him from the corner of my eye I catch him looking back at me, a little smile playing at his lips.

Solomon and Tanya join us, and we sit in a friendly silence. The fire throws sparks into the gaps between our conversation.

"I suppose they'll be at the fireside in Featherstone too right now," I say. "Ready for a meeting or a story or some food." I think back to those times we were all together in Featherstone. Some nights those meetings felt like one soul in many bodies; other times, it felt like the tension crackled louder than the flames.

"I don't know what stories they tell these days, what lies Sana shares." Solomon looks so sad and I remember that it was him I first heard tell a story around the fire – a story that was at once so familiar and so different it left me stunned. We ease back into the comfortable dream state that happens when you're around a fire – the hypnotic beauty, the feeling that nothing beyond your circle of light exists.

"Will you tell a story, Solomon?" I ask, and he smiles.

"Not I, Leora." The firelight brings out the smile lines on his face, and the worry lines. "I know you are here for a reason. If I want to hear any story tonight, it is the story of what brought you back – and what brought you out, storyteller." His dark eyes meet Mel's. "I have always wanted to hear a tale told by a true storyteller."

Mel looks at me and I nod. She sits cross-legged, her back tall and straight. Looking each of us in the eye as though sewing our souls together, she draws our attention tight, until all we see is her. Only then, does she begin.

They say that when you reach the heights the only way you can go is down. And so it seemed for Mayor Longsight. A young leader, cut from the same cloth as Saintstone's heroes. Mayor Longsight

had gained the love and trust of his people and, it seemed, even his enemies respected him.

Until one morning when the community gathered to watch as the mayor shared his latest success – a spy mission. He stood high on a podium – seen by all his people. They saw a woman in black scale the platform. They saw her plunge a blade beneath his ribs. They saw the flood of blood that spilled from their leader and they saw him fall.

When Mayor Longsight died, so too did his people's hope.

While their enemies rejoiced, the people of Saintstone mourned. The townspeople wore black and honoured their leader's memory by paying homage when his body was on display. They were held back by attendants, kept at a respectful distance, but many longed to run to him and wash his skin with their tears.

At the apportioned time, his skin was prepared and the mayor was ready to be taken to the flayers' for the next stage of his journey into eternity. But, then, it happened. His chest began to rise and fall, his fingers twitched, and his mouth moved – declaring all that he had learned from the ancestors while he was in the depths. Our leader, who had been dead, was now alive.

His advisor, Jack Minnow, instructed him to wait a few days until he was strong and then the miracle was announced. The frenzied joy of impossible wishes granted filled the town. This beloved leader was man no longer – he was something more – a victor, beater of the final enemy, lord over death.

Tanya – appalled and astonished – tries to speak, but Mel holds up a hand. This is her story and she will tell it to its end. We are transfixed; our storyteller's eyes reflect the flames of the fire and the heat in our hearts.

One miracle was not enough, however. It's funny how quickly things once hailed as wonders lose their shine. And acceptance is never satisfactory when what you really desire is worship. A stage was set, and the town's finest inker was summoned to mark the mayor. In a public ceremony the mayor was given a punishment mark in another man's place. The criminal's debt paid by the miracle man. But this work of humble sacrifice was not enough; one week later, the mayor appeared again before the people and he revealed his latest feat. The mark that was made – that was inked into his skin on behalf of another – that mark had completely disappeared.

Oscar draws in a breath – the air hissing through his teeth breaks the magic. Mel looks around at us and she is Mel again, not our storyteller. The rest of her words sound like a friend explaining to friends.

144

"His next sacrifice was to be on Leora's behalf. I can only imagine that he was intending to take on the crow – the mark of the forgotten. But he never got a chance because the meeting was interrupted. A most terrible thing occurred. A house was broken into and the skin books stolen.

"A skin book is the symbol of a soul that lives for ever – to steal one of these books is akin to a kidnapping; to destroy it would be murder. No one in Saintstone would commit such a heinous crime. But there are others who might." Her gaze rakes over them. "We know that Sana is behind this and we have come to stop her."

"She must be stopped," I say. My voice sounds tired. "Longsight's new teachings have, for the first time in years, distracted the people from their hatred of the blanks. If ever we were to broker for peace, it is now." I look to Mel, because there is more to the story – her dreams, the prophecy of the sisters, my rapidly cohering mark. But she shakes her head, ever so slightly. "Tomorrow we will visit Featherstone and we will be heard. Whether Sana will listen is another matter."

They are silent for a while, thinking. And then, at last, Tanya nods.

"If there is a chance for peace, then we must take it. But Sana is very far gone with her hatred. We know what she is capable of."

Mel nods. "And yet, we can but try." She rubs her eyes. "Leora, we must sleep – we have much work ahead of us."

"I'll take you to her myself, in the morning," Oscar says and stands. Mel raises an eyebrow and smiles at me.

"He's brave, your Oscar," she murmurs as we walk together towards our sleeping area.

And, as I lie there, I let those words swirl deliciously in my mind. *My Oscar.*

Chapter Twenty-five

The early morning in a forest is a strange time to be human. It is the time at which you are most aware that you don't belong – this territory is owned by the others. Birds trill and caw in a cloud of sound and squirrels are at their most brave. A fox waits us out along a path, standing its ground while we step by, all big feet and noise. A pheasant ignores us and a magpie flutters over our heads, the beats of its wings making my heart race.

Mel has been collecting twigs and sticks, putting them into her satchel as she walks. When we cross the stream, Mel passes the horse's reins to Oscar and, paying no attention to our confused faces, dips a bucket she brought from the camp to collect water. Oscar and I lead the horses while Mel walks, swaying with the weight of the bucket. We are close now, so very close.

Featherstone is still asleep when we arrive.

The sky is pink and scarlet when Mel walks up the slope towards the ever-burning fire. The bucket of water laps as she walks. When she reaches the top, she turns and looks down towards the village. With her feet planted, the pail of water in her hand and the fire raging behind her, she is the silhouette of a goddess: a flaming deity of warning and judgement.

The man who has been tending the fire through the night goes to Mel, but when he sees her skin he runs towards the settlement. Her marks are extraordinary in the firelight – the burnished tales of Saintstone. Her ink is like molten metal, like weapons being forged, like silver in the crucible. Like war, like peace.

Instead of the rallying, raging crowd I expect, there is a slow drip of curious souls that come and stand at the base of the hill, all the time watching Mel, Oscar and me warily.

The children are first.

Mel has not paused – she does not play for an audience; she has been busy. All the time since she placed the bucket on the ground, she has been taking twigs from her bag and setting them in pyramids. Soon the patch of ground where she stands is littered with these tiny structures, standing in pairs, carefully waiting.

The children draw near, hungry and curious. They have grown somewhat accustomed to marked faces, but this is something new – this is entertainment and they hold their breaths waiting to see what will happen next.

Still not speaking, not looking at any of the young faces gazing at her, Mel takes a stick from the fire and with her other hand she fills her water flask from the bucket. She walks around her creations and stops at each pair. One twig construction she lights with fire from the torch in her hand and the other she drenches with water. Each structure tumbles down and every time the children call out in amusement, frustration and distress at her studious destruction.

The parents have drawn closer by now, mistrustful of this marked stranger who plays with fire – entranced too by her methodical dance of fire and water.

Mel walks around once more, stamping out what remains of the tiny blazes, kicking at the muddy puddles of fallen twigs. The children don't know whether to join her or tell on her and their parents purse their lips in disapproval – and yet, no one interferes, nobody dares stop her.

The rest of the town are trudging up the hill now. And then I see that Sana is here, standing at the back of the crowd, arms crossed, head inclined, shoulders back – she is leader enough to allow this intrusion, her body says. But I know she is also leader enough to call for Mel's destruction. Seeing Sana chills me with fear and I hope that Mel is as certain of her actions as she seems.

Mel has placed the flaming branch back next to the fire and this time she takes sticks out of her bag – marginally longer than the twigs she has already used – and again, she builds. This time just two structures, side by side, and finally, she looks up as though noticing her audience for the first time and she straightens her shoulders, lifts her chin, shaking her red curls out of her face, and her story begins.

"Once there were two friends and the two friends built their houses next to each other." Mel puts the finishing touches to the two stick houses she has built. "'Now we are neighbours!' the friends said, and they were happy and glad."

The children look at each other and smile, already enjoying the story, feeling tickled to attend this surprise performance.

"But one day – a terrible day – there was a storm." Mel's eyes flash and the children squirm in delight at the promise of peril. "And on that terrible day the storm sent a fork of lightning and it struck one of the houses." At this, Mel reaches again for the flaming branch and touches it to the house on her right – each time making her voice rumble and crackle like thunder and lightning. One child cries out "No!" when he sees the house begin to burn. Flames lick at the twigs and already it begins to teeter. "And on that terrible day the storm sent rain and a flood swept up to the other house." Mel lifts the bucket and pours what is left of the water around the second twig house. The house falls immediately, and the water runs its way downward – the children shift to let the torrent pass and watch as the sticks that formed the house float down the hill, getting caught up in leaves and grass. One child catches a stick and returns it to Mel as though it might make the whole house come back again.

Mel looks down at her feet and every eye follows. On one side is a pile of charred wood and on the other is a pool with one lone stick lying in it. The children look at Mel with anger and suspicion. Where is the happy ending of the story? Surely there is more to come. Their agitated chatter halts as soon as Mel begins again.

"On this terrible day, fire destroyed one man's house and water destroyed the other. From that day on, each man made an oath. The man whose house was struck by lightning and burned to the ground vowed that he would never again let fire come close to him or his home. The man whose house was caught in the rain and swept away by a flood swore that he would never again let water come close to him or his home. Each man was determined.

"'Fire destroys,' the one man said. 'Water is deadly,' said the other. Each one said, 'Now I am safe.'"

The children start to raise their hands, whimpering with the urge to fix this tale, but Mel carries on.

"It was not long before each man became ill. One man wept because of his thirst but insisted, 'I will not allow water near me,' even though his tongue stuck to the roof of his dry mouth. The other man wept from hunger. He had meat and potatoes – indeed his table was laden with food, but he shouted, 'I will not allow fire near me,' and so the meat went rancid and the potatoes rotted, and he ate nothing."

I'm reminded of a dream I once had, a dream where the sisters were in separate cottages and each had what the other needed. I know how this story should end.

Mel picks up the stick that has been left in the deluge and prods at the mud and ash, making a mud-pie mush of the two houses. Making a mess.

"And so, both men dropped down dead." Mel releases the stick and shrugs.

The crowd are silent, even the children simply gape at Mel. But I see it in their eyes – she got it wrong. That's not how a story like this should end.

Chapter Twenty-six

A slow clap breaks the stunned, cold calm.

"Oh, very good." Sana paces slowly towards Mel, still with the sarcastic applause, each one sounding like a slap in the face. The sea of people parts before her. "A majestic performance – terribly moving." She treads over the mutilated parts of the houses Mel built, not caring to look down at the mess beneath her feet. "This is where we weep, where we cry out that if only the friends had shared, if only they weren't so stubborn. . ." Sana is small next to Mel, but she is like that fox we saw on our way – standing her ground, knowing this is her space and that we are merely trespassing. She is wiry and wily; we underestimate her at our peril.

The rest of the community press in on us now. Mel no longer holds the fort. Hers was a momentary dominion, and now the power has been reclaimed; children return to their parents and eye Mel with suspicion.

"That's what you're saying, yes?" Sana continues. "If

only the blanks and the marked weren't so *obstinate*. If they could just see that the one way for them both to survive was to work together." She raises an eyebrow. "You'll tell me if I've got it wrong?" Mel says nothing. "Message received, storyteller."

I risk a look at Oscar and see the tension in his face too. We are both poised to run. Mel however is stately and utterly fearless. She looks at Sana without pity or hatred and I can hardly believe it when I see that, shining from her face, is love.

"Sana, we got *your* message," Mel says. "Loud and clear. You know how to hit us where it will cause us the most pain. To have a skin book taken away is like losing a lover. Clever girl." Sana shrugs. "But your attack was futile. It came at a time when the people's antagonism towards your community is at its lowest. The citizens of Saintstone have moved on – they have passed on the opportunity to fight. Now is time for something else, something new. There is a chance for hope here. Have mercy on your people. Call for peace."

"And this is the word of who – Minnow?" Sana smirks.

"This is the word of a friend." Mel looks around at me and Oscar. "Believe me, you do not want to wait until Mayor Longsight sends word."

"Mayor Longsight? Don't be a fool, storyteller. Longsight's long gone."

"He's alive, Sana," I call out, and she looks up, narrowing her eyes at me.

"No – no. He is dead. I made sure. . ." Her rage and confusion make her incautious. There is a ripple through the crowd of people – Oscar will have told them what Sana did, but I wonder how many truly believe she was his killer.

"He died." Mel's voice is melodious and calm. "But he is alive again. He is an object of worship, Sana – his word holds more sway than ever before, and the people love him and serve him even more faithfully."

Sana looks about her, at me, at Oscar and Mel, and finally at her people. She smooths out the astonished shock that lines her face and smiles out at the jumble of townsfolk who look on.

"These inked fools will believe anything," Sana scoffs, addressing her followers. "They come here with their delusions, telling us to seek peace. Just look at them, look at how well-fed they are, look at their clothes and their boots which fit and have not been repaired fifteen times over. They think peace is when we blanks shut our hungry mouths. When we stop fighting for our land. That is servitude, not peace, and it is certainly not justice." Sana spits at Mel's feet, who takes a step back. "You have wasted your time, storyteller. And the irony is," her voice rises and there is a strange undercurrent, underneath the scorn – something manic, strange, "the irony is that in the time you have spent here, setting up your little houses, telling your quaint story, my crew have been riding hard, bound for Saintstone. You came here to build your houses and tell your tale while my riders are in your home weighing out justice. For we are the fire and water; we are the lightning and flood." She laughs, and it echoes around the hillside. "Run home, little children, and see what is left of the houses you built."

I take another look at the crowd and I see that the riders, Sana's own most faithful lackeys, are not here. Fenn is not here. She's not making it up, then – they are in Saintstone reaping destruction and we are powerless to stop them.

Not everyone cheers, but those who do are loud and fearsome. I look around for a friendly face, someone who might be kind. I see Kasia, her expression full of dread, and I see Penny and Blake – Penny's baby must be due so soon. They cower at the edge, looking terrified and miserable, as though they long to help us but know they must first protect themselves. Penny mouths the word, but it's Blake I hear – he screams at us: "Run!"

Chapter Twenty-seven

We race to where the horses are tethered, with Sana's mocking laughter echoing in our ears, Oscar refuses to mount, saying we mustn't let him slow us down. Before we can protest, he slaps the horses and we pelt through the woods.

We slow only when we're on the furthest edge.

"We won't be in time to stop them," I pant, and Mel nods, wiping her sweat-slicked forehead. She takes a look behind us, trying to gauge whether or not we are being followed. Eventually she sighs, her face taut with misery, and we ride on, in time with our heavy breaths.

"Will they be all right?" I ask. I'm thinking of our friends and neighbours. Of Mum. All unprepared for an attack.

"I don't know," says Mel. She looks taut with worry. "Minnow is a good leader. He will protect his people."

Interesting, I think, that she mentions Minnow rather than Longsight. I have often wondered about them – they seem so different and yet both have fought for the same thing for so long.

"How well do you know Jack Minnow?" I ask, and Mel takes a while to answer.

"I've known him since I was a small child – from when I started being mentored for my calling; he had just begun work with the government. A school leaver mentorship, I suppose. He's maybe ten years older than me. He was the brooding guy I liked when I was thirteen."

I can't help but laugh – it's hard to imagine her as a teenager with a crush.

"But we only met properly when I was instated as storyteller after my mentor died. He's always been quite reserved, you know? Of course, our paths cross all the time now."

"You don't still like him . . . like *that*?" I ask, horrified.

"Your face!" Mel laughs at me. "But no. I don't get to have romantic relationships or marry. One of the rules."

"Is that lonely?" I ask. "I don't think I would like to be told whether or not I could fall in love."

"Ah, there are no rules about falling in love." Mel's face has a distracted, faraway look. "And love doesn't always look the way you expect it."

"Did you know that Jack Minnow visits the hall of remembrance every night?" I ask, but Mel doesn't reply.

"I followed him." This at least gets a reaction – a raised eyebrow and an amused smile.

"You really ought to respect other people's mourning," Mel tells me, ever the good mentor.

"Anyway, he was saying someone's name over and over again, and for some reason I know it was someone who wasn't supposed to be remembered. A forgotten."

"Davey Minnow?" asks Mel immediately and I stare at her.

"Davey Minnow," I reply. "Family, obviously?" She says nothing. "Why was he forgotten?"

She smiles at me. "You want me to tell you everything?"

"That would be nice," I say. "It would certainly make it easier than me trying to subtly lead the conversation that way."

"You are not subtle, Leora. You have many great gifts, but subtlety? No. Even without the ability to read marks, it's not too hard to read your face."

"Well, we can't all be mysterious, Mel." I laugh.

"OK. So, Davey Minnow was one of the crows."

My head snaps to look at Mel – she's not joking.

"He was an important member of the group, as far as I can gather. One of the original leaders."

"This... I wasn't expecting you to tell me that. Why would a member of Minnow's family have joined the crows?"

"I can't know for sure. The resettlement wasn't as easy for the people of Saintstone as the school textbooks would have you believe." I nod, thinking back to the terrible things Ruth and Sana told me. "Davey Minnow, Jack's father, would have been in the generation that followed the resettlement, a time when memories were still fresh. The rumour is that members of the Minnow family were among those who were sent to Featherstone."

"You think members of Minnow's family might have been blank?"

"I don't know – I'm just saying it's a possibility. Maybe that's why Davey Minnow joined the crows – to help them. Or he could have just been a man with a heart."

"Not much family resemblance, then," I say sourly.

"I know you hate him, but Jack Minnow is as human as you. It's like anything – anyone," she says. "If you know their story, it's much harder to hate them."

"You say that, but you're no different – all your life you wouldn't listen to the blanks. You wouldn't hear their story."

She nods. "Absolutely. I thought I had the whole story. And I was wrong – blind. I thought I was protecting our people. It's not a great excuse. But people change. I have changed, and I hope that gives you some hope."

She is quiet for a moment, thinking, and then she says, "One night, many years ago when we were both young and he had too much to drink, Jack told me that he had once accompanied his father on a mission with the crows, to bring the blanks food and drink. He was very young, just a boy. He talked of conversations around a fire, of companionship between blank and marked. His face was soft, as though the memory was a happy one."

It occurs to me, at last, that this is how Jack Minnow and Sana know each other. Sana told me about blanks and crows meeting in the forest; of course their paths would have crossed, a friendship forged.

I imagine Minnow and Sana as children, sitting on stones around a fire, sharing stories while the adults danced. I can just hear Sana telling Jack the story she told me – her favourite tale, of the lovers, the king who staged his death and believed in his own resurrection. I wonder. Not for the first time, I wonder why Minnow told Sana that there would be a public meeting that day in the square. He must have known she couldn't resist the theatre of an assassination, in front of all Longsight's people – an attack just when they were boasting of their strength. *Why?* I think. *Why?*

"I think he loved those days," Mel says. "He would hate me to say it – but I think he enjoyed being part of the crows and was proud of his father, until..."

"Yes?" I urge.

"Jack's father – Davey Minnow – was killed." Mel's brow furrows.

"What happened?"

"There are a number of stories. Some crows said he died in the forest of a sudden heart attack. Others think he was hijacked by the leaders of Saintstone – that his death was a warning to the crows that they must stop their support of the blanks. Jack Minnow, however, believes his father was killed by the blanks. That certain rebels within the blank community hated even the crows for being marked and made an example of him. Whatever the truth of it, those joyful gatherings ended when Davey Minnow died.

"The crows brought his body home – a miserable and treacherous journey. The dead are a heavy weight to carry."

Carrying the corpse through the dank air of the woods. I try not to think about it.

"Jack refused to have anything to do with the crows from then on, and now I suspect no one knows he was ever involved. I am probably the only one. If Mayor Longsight knew, he would reconsider his blind trust of Jack. And, as for why Jack risks it all and goes to the hall of remembrance each night? Well, Davey Minnow never had a weighing of the soul ceremony. He was forgotten."

That word, *forgotten*, still stuns my soul.

Sometimes when I think about Dad I can only remember what he was like at the end, and the guilt I feel for that weighs me down like a million white stones. He's not that wrinkled man who could hardly speak, whose breath smelled of decay and whose eyes were frozen lakes. He is more than that – a lifetime more. A lifetime of his laugh, his voice telling me a story or teasing Mum. His fingernails cut neat and short for his work; his broad, capable hands. The hands that held mine when I was learning how to cross roads; that held mine when I wanted him to show me how to draw; the hands that held on so tightly when he knew he was going to die. It always comes back to that – my thoughts and memories always reach the end point, no matter how much I try to send them back to the beginning. It is that whole life that needs to be remembered. I still yearn to find his book and read it again. Maybe Mel will help me, like she said.

Jack Minnow is not that different from me. His father a crow, by all accounts a good man. And yet. . .

If the injustice of his father's death and status as forgotten has been eating him from within all this time, no wonder Jack Minnow has barely anything left of his own soul.

Chapter Twenty-eight

The closer we get to Saintstone, the more we pick up our pace. We both dread what we will find on our return.

It is the middle of the night by the time we arrive, and the echo of our horses' hoof beats is all I hear; there is no screaming, no weeping, no sound of battle or destruction. We walk with our horses and return them to stables that are empty, the sounds of them drinking and the clinking and creaking of tack being removed, the sweep of brushes – they are all so loud against the backdrop of quiet that it feels conspicuous. On foot, we head to the centre of the town, treading carefully as though we are creeping up on our prey.

Homes are shut up as usual, sleepy and calm, and I begin to wonder whether Sana has tricked us after all. But then we walk around the corner into the square, and we stop.

Two golden-robed readers walk away from the hall of remembrance, their heads down and their steps unsteady.

Their robes are even more flame-like tonight, with ash and scorches at their hems. The hall itself is quiet and the doors are open, not because the building is in use as it has been day and night since the town's memory began, but because the huge wooden doors have been torn from their hinges like broken teeth in a beautiful face. The boiled-sweet glass panes that blinked rainbows on to the town square have been smashed, and I realize why the townspeople are not here – there is nothing left for them to fight for. The town is dead because one of the chambers of its heart has been destroyed.

Mel stands with me at the entrance, but when I step forward she takes my hand.

Tears stream down her face and she shakes her head. "I can't," she whispers, and I nod.

"I must," I reply.

We hold on to each other for a long time, our bodies shaking together in fear and anguished sobs. Before she goes, Mel whispers to me: "Leora, go and see your mother. They lied to you about her." Away she whips into the darkness and I am alone.

I look all around to check that I am not being watched or followed, but only silence crouches behind the corners of buildings. I walk in freely.

Some of the seats have scorch marks over them – burned but not destroyed. *Lucky*, I think for a second, but then I wonder whether it would have been better if the whole building had been lost to fire because this sight is agony.

The quiet is the worst thing: the alien silence in a space that has always, *always* held the whispers of the names of the worthy. The only pause was at the brief beat of a breath taken – a pause readying the next wave of words. But the readers have gone, and their voices have been silenced, and now who will say the names of the long dead who deserve to be remembered for eternity? They did well, Sana's riders – they have taken the ceremony of remembrance from us, and without memory we are nothing.

I walk slowly towards the front of the building and almost trip over burned ropes. I shudder when I wonder whether the readers were tied up and made to watch the destruction of this sacred space. Their howls almost echo in the silence of the broken hall. The book of the dead has been destroyed, and if they were made to watch, it must have been like watching a murder. I should know.

When I reach the dais I stop, feeling as though I should kneel or pray or at the very least, weep, but I am silent. Glass crackles under my feet and my nostrils fill with the scent of burned wood and spilled incense.

"A risky move, coming here."

My blood turns to ice.

He's always waiting in the shadows. I don't turn to look at him. I keep my eyes on the lectern.

"Minnow," I sigh. The hairs on my arms prickle to gooseflesh when I hear him walk closer. I can smell his soap – a leather-mint fragrance. He stops next to me, his arm touching mine – the heat from him seeping out towards me. From the edge of my vision I see him raise his face to the beamed ceiling. We stand in silence.

"This was the blanks. This was an act of evil." I break the silence with the words I've been wanting to say since I walked in.

Minnow lets out a whisper of a laugh.

"At last, you admit they can do wrong."

I don't like his mockery. I hate that even now he is closed and stone-like. I want him to break.

"What will you do now that you can't say your father's name in this place?" I say, and I hear his sharp, indrawn breath. I should be afraid. I should be running. But I stay, and my heart does not race, and my breath does not grow heavy. "Not all those who are forgotten are guilty. I know you whisper your father's name: Davey Minnow. I know he deserves to be in the book of the dead." I toe a scrap of parchment that lies on the ground. "We're not so different after all."

We wait, standing side by side. I don't know for how long, but I'm sure I hear birdsong.

"Will this just go on for ever?" I say, looking at where the book lies in burned tatters. "The blanks attack and we retaliate? Haven't you grown tired of all this – the hatred and division and death? Will we repay death with more death or will we redeem it and bring people to life while we still can?" He is still. Jack Minnow is terribly, masterfully still. "There's time, Jack. My dad would have wanted me to live and flourish. I don't know what your dad wanted for you, but I'm sure it wasn't this."

"Compassion killed my father," he says. "You can't live long if you have a weak heart – one that is soft to everything." He lets the pause spool out and when he speaks again his voice is soft. "I intend to live."

We stay there, shoulder to shoulder until something behind us scuttles and we both turn, tensing. It's a crow. Flustered and flapping, stuck in the building after finding its way in somehow. We gaze at it, watch it slam against windows. After a minute the bird moves, and, drawn by slow dawn light peeping through empty window frames, it gets lucky – a broken window: red, blue and green glass lost to the stones. The crow flits through it and, with a shriek, is free.

Minnow and I walk side by side through the doors. He turns left, I turn right, and the crow soars above us.

Chapter Twenty-nine

I told Dad that painting a house on the rock where we hid the spare key was a ridiculous idea.

"Why don't you just write a sign saying 'Burglars: help yourselves!'?" I said, rolling my eyes.

"Where's your sense of magic, little light?" He had grinned at me. "This is a fairy house." He lifted up the delicately decorated rock for me to see. "You'll see; they'll take care of our key." I shook my head and told him he'd regret it, but the key always stayed in place and no one ever broke in. But now there are skin book stealers on the prowl, and no amount of fairy magic could protect us from Sana's plans.

The rock is heavier than I remember and woodlice scuttle away when I move it. A spider stands guard and seems to step aside when I reach down and pick up the key between thumb and finger. The key is cold and muddy, scales of rust beginning to show at the bow, but it is there: I'm going back home.

I ease the door open as quietly as possible. There is someone on the sofa – or, at least, the shadow of someone. They are black and grey, like a memorial tattoo, and it's only when she says my name that I realize it's my mum. But she's not the woman I left when I went to Featherstone; she's not the mother who told me, "Just do what you have to do to stay safe." She's a bad sketch, a crumpled picture thrown away. And the starkest difference grips me tightly around the throat: across her face is a fierce slash of black ink – a diagonal cheekbone-to-jaw tear that cuts across her nose. She has been tattooed with a mark I've never seen before and I can't help but read her, for this mark screams violence and disgrace. It is all pain and punishment. This mark has left her lonely, afraid and all but forgotten.

I had wondered what I was going to say. But there's no space for words. I kneel at her feet and she cups my face in her hands. With the soft pad of her thumb she wipes my tears away and kisses my cheeks. I reach up and touch the mark on her face, and she closes her eyes in hurt and shame. I rise and plant three soft kisses across the ink. She takes my hand, and she leads me upstairs.

I am home.

My bedroom has been left untouched since I left, and Mum insists on tucking me in. But I can't sleep, and after a while I creep into her bed and fall asleep with her holding on to my hand.

I dream I am cradling a baby. I stand at the riverside listening to the whisper of wind in the reeds, the rush of the water as it laps over rocks. The baby makes no sound when I lay it in the box. I do not nail the box shut — for this baby is no king. I don't want it to return in three days and be made a god. No, this baby who smiles at me from their basket must not come back. Not until the time is right.

"Don't be a king or queen," I whisper. "Don't be a miracle maker."

I lift the basket and set it down in the reeds, watching as the water sucks it into the current, and as the basket floats away on the wild waters I call out.

"Be brave, be good. Be free of these dreams and stories and fights. Know peace, and if you find it, bring it back. But not yet. Not yet. . ."

And the baby in the basket laughs as it floats downstream.

"They said you didn't want to see me," I tell Mum in the morning as we sit at our wooden kitchen table and sip black tea. She has no milk in the house, no bread or butter for toast. "Mayor Longsight told me. It was my fault, Mum – I'm so sorry I left you to pick up all the broken pieces I left behind."

"Oh, Leora, when will you learn not to believe a word that man tells you?" This, from Mum, shocks me – she has always been the good one, the one who knew the rules and obeyed. She's never spoken about the town's leader like that.

"When you left, people were wonderful – I was so cared for and supported. My true friends knew there was more to it than the story that was being told." A small smile crinkles the corners of Mum's eyes.

"So, what changed?" I ask tentatively. I look around the kitchen. It is bare and shabby. This is not the house of someone who is being cared for.

"Mayor Longsight hated what he saw: his people showing greater loyalty to the ties of friendship than to him." Mum's usually clear voice is gravelled and croaky. She sips her tea. "So, he took charge of the situation." She swallows, shifting in the seat.

"Your mark?" I ask, and she nods.

"Sometimes I think the man is just a fool and then he goes and does something so calculated..." She sighs. "I was made an example of at one of his public markings. He announced it like it was a game. There was a new type of mark, he told the people, a tattoo that was called the mark of loyalty. The people were excited, but he told them he hoped that it would be a rare mark – made only on those who truly deserved it. They dragged me up to the stage." She tries to keep her voice light, but as she pushes her hair out of her eyes, I see her hand shake. "He announced that thus far, only I had earned the loyalty mark. That it was a mark used to alert others – a warning for the truly loyal. He told them my sins: that I had married a man who fraternized with blanks, that I had raised a blank child, that I had lived an entire life in scorn of the purity of Saintstone. He said that I had tricked them all: deceived them. Led people astray without their knowing. My friends, my clients, my fellow readers, those who sold me food and clothes – all this time, they had been shoulder to shoulder with a criminal. It was not their fault, he said; they weren't to know.

"He told them I would not be marked as forgotten. He made it sound like such grace. He gave me the chance to escape punishment by publicly disowning you." She shakes her head as though the idea is nonsense. "They marked me there and then." Mum looks right into my eyes. "Leora, it was agony. It was fire like I've never felt in my life. And now wherever I go, this mark goes too. I haven't been served at the market since."

I reach out and hold her hand.

"But your friends? Surely. . ."

"There is too much to lose. If any of them are seen with me, they will be marked in this way too – he said so. I wouldn't wish this on any of them; I don't blame them for not coming."

Her voice is strong, but her face is so sad. I hate Longsight all the more today. I hate him for letting me believe that my mum would stop loving me and I hate him most of all for doing this to her. He has made her invisible.

A light knock on the back door sets my heart racing, but Mum waves a hand at me and goes to open it. At the door, holding a paper bag in his arms, is the last person I imagined seeing: Seb – Verity's older brother, a young man with a learning disability who has been in my life since before I can remember. His familiar face is almost too much for me after the past few weeks. I rush over and hurl my arms around him, crushing the bag between us.

"Seb! What are you doing here?"

He grins at me and walks past, placing the bag on the table. He turns back and opens his arms to me so we can hug again, properly.

"What am *I* doing here? What about you?" he says. He bends to look at me right in the face and ruffles my hair. "You're trouble, Leora Flint," he tells me, his face mock-grave, and then he laughs and hugs me all over again.

"I am trouble, you're right," I tell him when we finally let each other go. "And it's really risky for you to be here."

"Seb's a grown-up," Mum says. "He doesn't need you mithering him. Besides, he and I have had the same conversation a million times. He's a stubborn bugger, and he's the reason I'm still alive."

She tells me it began with Seb bringing the loaves leftover at the end of the day at the bakery where he works.

"They were going to throw them in the bin, so I took them," he says.

"Then, it turns out that Seb is such a charmer that people give him things wherever he goes." Mum laughs.

He's unpacking the bag and I see fruit, a small bag of sweets, a glass bottle of milk and some wine. Seb lifts the bottle to show me. "Employee of the month, *again*." As though he is tired of being brilliant.

I can't stop laughing.

"Seb, you are a hero," I tell him, shaking my head in wonder.

"I know." He grins.

Chapter Thirty

While Seb cuts biscuit dough, he tells us what happened after the sacking of the hall of remembrance.

"It happened last night. It was awful. When we got to the hall it was destroyed. The blanks were gone before the guard knew what had happened." He shakes his head. "The readers all got out safely. Then there was another meeting in the square first thing this morning. All the people were shouting. The mayor said that he would take care of us – and there's going to be another marking soon."

I frown. *Something is missing here*, I think.

"So, what are they going to do to retaliate?" I ask. "What's Mayor Longsight going to do to punish the blanks?"

Rolling out the offcuts of dough and scattering flour on the surface with a practised flourish, Seb shrugs. "That's what the people in the crowd were shouting. They shouted so loud, I didn't like it." Mum rubs his shoulder. "They calmed down a bit when Jack Minnow spoke instead. The people clapped him."

I wait while Seb carefully puts the tray of biscuits in the oven.

"Seb, what else did Minnow say?" I ask.

"He made an announcement. A big one. Some more books got stolen and so he says everyone has to bring their skin books to the museum, so they can be guarded and kept safe."

Seb is so matter-of-fact that it takes a while for his words to sink in.

"You mean, all the books that people have in their houses – all the skin books – are going to be kept in the museum?"

Seb nods. "Yep, so they'll be safe." He brushes his hands clean and takes off the apron he is wearing. "Those biscuits will be ready when the timer goes, but leave them to cool before you try and move them." Seb gives us both giant hugs and leaves through the back door.

Mum is smiling fondly, but my heart is racing. Without the skin books in their homes people will have no access to their family – no means by which to carry the daily ritual so many perform: lighting of a candle, greeting by name. It may be protection for the books, but from the outside, locked doors will always seem like a prison.

"They're taking people's books." My words tremble

under my effort to remain calm. "Not the blanks – the *government*."

"It sounds awful, I know," Mum says, "but what else can they do? At least by keeping them at the museum they are all in one place. They can guard them."

"The people are losing everything," I try and explain. "The hall of remembrance is gone. The readers cannot work and so the dead cannot be mourned. And now the family skin books get taken away. How are people supposed to honour their loved ones now?"

"At least they have their loved ones to honour." Her chin flies up and her eyes are bright with anger. "At least ... at least people will eventually get their family's books back once this has passed. Your father is gone for ever. I will never hold him again."

"Oh, Mum." I pull her into my arms and rub her back. I can't stop worrying about what Seb said.

Mayor Longsight's reticence to respond to the latest attack really troubles me. Not that I want more conflict – retaliation can only mean innocent people being hurt. What bothers me is how out of character it seems. Since he was sworn in as mayor he has been claiming to be a "back to the old ways" kind of leader; it all made so much sense: all our problems were because we were neglecting our roots, our religion and ritual. We had become lax and let our standards as the marked slip. Longsight promised us that purity would lead to stability, wealth and happiness.

A crackdown on soft attitudes towards the blanks was part of that. I thought war was on the horizon. His weak words today feel like when a teacher would tell me to ignore a bully – as though that might stop them trying to trip me up whenever I walked past. It's one thing ignoring things that don't exist, but to act as though the shocking attack on the hall of judgement was nothing . . . well, it's dangerously unaware. The only thing that has changed is Longsight and this new teaching he's supposed to have received. It's as though all he cares about is proving his greatness, and yet. . . I can't imagine his glib response has increased his popularity.

I pull back from Mum and look at her weary face.

"When's the last time you left the house?"

She looks at me stonily. "The last time I went out, I saw the mayor killed. I had my purple shawl and I hoped no one would see me."

"I saw you," I say. I remember the purple scarf, but not her mark – she must have hidden it well. "You can't give in – you deserve to live. You're not in the jail so why are you imprisoning yourself?"

"I'm not brave like you, love," she says quietly. "Why would I go out there, when I know everyone hates me?"

"Seb likes you."

Mum manages a small smile.

"Only Seb. Not even Julia has come since I was marked. It's like I don't exist – like I've already been forgotten."

Julia is Verity's mum and Mum's oldest friend. I can't believe she would abandon her like this, that only her son has the bravery to remain loyal. "Don't say that," I tell her firmly and she seems to shrink. I sigh and go to hug her again. "I'm not brave," I murmur into her ear. "I am scared all the time. You know that Longsight and Minnow would love it if I just . . . disappeared. But that's not what we're here for – what would Dad say?"

Mum holds me away from her and looks into my face, shaking her head.

"Oh, Leora, he would say so many things." She takes a breath. "He would say he's proud of you." I roll my eyes. "And he would tell us we're crows now." She laughs. "He always wanted me to join – maybe it's time."

"I think you'd have to leave the house for that." I smile. "Who are they, anyway? Why haven't they been helping you?"

"That's my own fault," Mum admits. "I burned bridges with them long ago – I was so angry with your father for joining them. It was so risky. I contacted Connor when I thought they might help us with your dad's book but look where that's got us. Anyway, after that I told them I never wanted anything to do with any of them." Her face looks like it did when she'd tell me off when I was small – tightly pinched.

The sound of the timer breaks our connection and Mum opens the oven. A waft of warm sweetness fills the room.

"Well," I say. "I'm going into town." I hold up a hand at Mum's horror-struck face. "You're welcome to join me, or I'll see you later."

Just as I close the front door I see her pick up a biscuit, but it cracks and drops on to the floor before she gets a morsel into her mouth. Should have listened to Seb.

Chapter Thirty-one

My confidence stalls once I'm walking. The last time I took this familiar route to the town square I hadn't yet visited Featherstone. It seems a lifetime ago. This is the way I used to go when I was working at the studio with Obel, heading to the museum with Dad, or going with Mum to the hall of remembrance. Nothing's like it used to be.

I turn on to the cobbled street hemmed in by terraced houses either side and, in spite of the warmth of the day, I wrap my shawl more tightly about me, shielding my face. Longsight had said I wasn't a prisoner, but he had me under control then – what would happen if he saw me walking freely? I need to see Mel, though.

Wilting flowers outside the florist offer a pungent punch as I enter the town square. Everyone is queuing to have their family's skin books taken into the care of the government. Arms are weighed down by boxes and bags, which are filled with the souls of their loved ones; hearts are heavy and shoulders droop. Every one of them will be feeling sicker and sadder the closer they get to incarcerating their family.

Tear-filled eyes don't see a girl with her scarf wrapped high at her neck as she scales the steps to the museum. My confident gait doesn't attract attention – all staff are focused on the books arriving and I walk past the reception desk without being noticed or stopped. It's as easy as looking purposeful.

I knock on Mel's door, waiting for her call to enter, but there is no answer and I let myself in, thinking that she must be assisting with the book amnesty and intending to wait a while. But when I step into the study, I know something is wrong.

Her chair has been tipped on its side and there is an upturned teacup on her desk, dregs of tea spilled across a book.

"Mel?" I call gently, shutting the door behind me. I check her bathroom, but it's empty. I cross the room and enter her bedroom; her covers are neat, her bag from our travels on the floor at the foot of her bed. And on her bed is the notebook with the marbled cover. My stomach plunges. I grab the notebook. Mel's gold pen is tucked between the pages, and I pause. I sit on her bed and open the notebook where the pen marks the page. A list – neat bullet points that speak of someone with plans and trouble sleeping.

- _Book_ a meeting with Mayor Longsight re: support from Moreton
- _Found_ someone's ring, must remember to pass on to lost property
- _Was_ I meant to be doing a school visit soon?? Check with Mrs Oldham
- _Seen_ a couple of books on wrong shelves recently – talk to librarian
- _Look_ for suitable candidates for the mayor's new marking protocol
- _Down_ to my last working pen – must get more

It's just a list, but my eyes run down it again – the first word of each line is underlined, ever so faintly. Again, I scour the page . . . until it clicks.

Book found. Was seen. Look down.

I get off the bed and on to my knees and reaching my hand under the bed my fingertips brush something – something smooth and chunky. I get lower, slide my arm in until it won't go any further. With painful slowness, I claw the item closer until I can slip it from its hiding place.

Dusty and scuffed, it takes a moment for me to process what I hold in my hands. It's Dad's skin book. Mel must have gone for it before she went back to her room last night. I hold it reverently and brush away the dirt with my sleeve. I turn each page and it's really him – every mark is like hearing his voice again after a hundred years. Mel did this. She saved him for me.

But at what cost?

Chapter Thirty-two

I walk out of the museum, attempting the same brisk, purposeful stride I used when I went in. The square is still full, and most people have their hands free now – skin books deposited into their temporary home at the museum. They have their attention elsewhere, and I look towards the stage, where everyone else seems to be focused. *Another public meeting*, I think.

But there is just one worker hanging a banner. They work from the left, lacing the edges against the front of the stage with ropes. I stand and look as they slowly unfurl the rolled fabric, wondering what new pronouncement Longsight is making this time. The worker is methodical, making sure not to crease the material or hang the banner askew. Slowly the words come into view.

WANTED
Leora Flint
On suspicion of the murder of the storyteller, Mel.

Cries of distress explode around the square like firecrackers. I blink and read the words again. My mind is screaming at me to run but I am paralysed by that cold, terrible word: murder.

Finally, my feet respond to my mind's pleas and I walk out of the square, down the cobbled street until I am far enough away to run. And I run home, all the time expecting the chase to begin.

"She can't be dead, Mum. Tell me – tell me she's not." I sob into Mum's firm embrace. No one is immune to the curse that I bring – if I love you, you may as well give up. But Mel? She was different. Mel was the strong one, the leader, the one who had been groomed to be part of the government since she was a child. She was courageous enough to take risks and not worry, because she was too important – she was safe.

"You're not going to leave me too, are you?" I whimper, and Mum tells me the comforting lies I need to hear.

"I'll never leave you. I'm here, and I'm staying right here." She murmurs softly into my hair.

Her words are soft and sweet, and they draw me in – I want the warmth of their promise; but like Seb's biscuits they could crumble at any moment.

They come and knock on the door and ask Mum whether I am here. They even commit a cursory search. I wait in my childhood hiding place: the big, dusty chest in the attic.

After they leave, Mum begs me to rest for a while, to stay till the next morning, to work out what we can do. I agree, to soothe her, and eventually she falls asleep, her hair tumbled on the pillow.

It feels like a long time since I picked up a pencil and drew. By the light of my bedside table lamp, I sit cross-legged on my bed and open Mel's notebook, sniffing back tears and smoothing the paper before I make a mark. I need to think, and to think, I need to draw. Around the new story of the sisters which Mel received, I let the nib play. The sisters sit together, and their stories begin to dance.

At first the images jar and clang in discord like the two versions of their history the sisters share. At one side a father smiles and his fingers curl softly around the song the little girl sings. On the other side is a monstrous man who thunders until the tiny girl at the edge of the page quakes. As the sister's stories grow and settle, harmony begins to be seen. I draw the branches of a tree behind their cottage – the boughs splay from the trunk as though making space from each other, and then the branches slowly draw close and eventually intertwine, until the pencil strokes become oceans of silken hair – black and pale blond, braided into wave after wave of perfectly united strands.

If the banner in the town square told one lie – that I am a killer – could it have told another? Is it possible that Mel is alive? There are a thousand reasons why it would be better for Mayor Longsight and Jack Minnow if Mel was dead. She knows so much about them both, too much. She has been their confidante and their equal – she is full of their secrets. Little wonder they wanted to silence her. But, until I see a body – unless I see the flayed skin of the storyteller – I won't let it be true. It doesn't change how things stand, because dead or alive, Mel would expect me to fight.

Wiping my tears, I tiptoe downstairs and collect Dad's book from my bag. I put it on Mum's bed, next to her pillow. He will be the first thing she sees when she wakes.

Chapter Thirty-three

I dream of untangling a ball of wool.

I dream of trying to find the right key on a ring of hundreds.

I dream of separating sugar from salt.

I dream of ice melting and refreezing.

I dream of a man who becomes a god and then becomes a man again and again and again.

I wake up before dawn, determined. My problem has been that the rules changed, and I've not caught up yet; I've been playing the wrong game entirely. I've been trying to understand the old Mayor Longsight – the one for whom power meant domination. He made sense to me – he wanted to lead by being the strongest, the wisest, the best and most fierce. So, of course, the destruction of the blanks was his aim. What better way to show his might and to declare his new intentions?

But now he is a new man – this "resurrection" has changed him. For him, power now looks like purity of soul, and he is the one with the keys to that particular door. He has made himself the only way. His is a promise of certainty. Of eternity.

Whatever doubts I have about Longsight's miracles – his resurrection and his taking away of another's ink – I realize that the most important thing isn't what I believe: it's what Mayor Longsight himself believes. And there is no disciple more faithful than him; he believes in himself even more than the flatterer Jack Minnow.

But I have a secret, a secret I've been holding in my hand – the truth about Jack Minnow. I'm ready to raise the stakes.

When Seb next visits he frowns at me.

"Did you hurt Mel?"

"Seb, I promise you. I haven't hurt or killed Mel – she is ... was ... my friend."

"Verity says you don't care about friends," Seb says matter-of-factly as he unpacks his latest offering of food. "She says you only care about yourself."

I try to swallow back tears, but Seb looks into my eyes and envelopes me in a hug.

"Verity cries too," Seb says, holding me tight. "You're my friend, Leora. That's why I help you and your mum."

"You're an incredible friend, Seb. And I'm trying to fix things."

Seb brushes a tear from my cheek. I wish it was safe for him to give Verity a message from me, but it would be reckless – dangerous. But, an idea sparks in my mind. Seb must see it because he says, "What? What are you thinking about?"

"You're good at passing on messages, aren't you?" I ask.

"I'm very good. Especially secret messages." He grins proudly. "No one expects me to have secrets." I laugh.

"If I gave you a message, would you make sure it got to the right person? You don't have to. You can say no and I won't mind."

He thinks for a moment. "Who should I take it to?" he says with a smile.

"Do you know Karl Novak?" I ask and Seb nods. "Could you get a note to him?"

"That's easy," Seb says. "He comes into the bakery on his way to work every day."

"So, you'll do it?"

"I'll do it tomorrow. Don't worry – you can count on me."

The note I give to Seb doesn't require a reply. I just have to hope that I am right to trust Karl. But then, I don't have any other choice.

Chapter Thirty-four

The breeze is chilly despite the early morning sun; I need my shawl for warmth as well as disguise. I asked Karl to meet me outside the studio, and shivering in the shady alleyway, I can only hope that he will come.

I don't have to wait long. When he turns the corner and stands silhouetted at the top of the passage, I remember our first day here at the studio. The sight of him had made my stomach lurch. But this morning, I could hug him.

He doesn't say anything, just gives me a tight nod, and then we start walking.

"You're sure about this?" Karl asks as he ushers me towards a side entrance to the government building. "You're wanted for murder – it seems foolish, to say the least, to be heading right for one of the people you're meant to be hiding from."

"I know. And it *is* foolish. But it might be the only way I can find out what's going on – and change things." I look up at Karl, his swept-back blond hair as neat as ever. He makes such a good government official; he looks the part, it's hard to believe he is on the side of the crows now. But I have to trust him – and even if he can't be trusted, all I need is to see Minnow face-to-face. "I didn't kill Mel, you know that, right?"

Karl sighs out a laugh. "Yes. I know that."

"Do you have any idea what happened to her?" I push.

He looks carefully at me. "Of course I have an idea. This is not the first time the leaders have called for someone to go 'missing'. But this is the first time I've not seen a body."

"You seem so different, Karl." I can't help it, I want to know. "What changed – what made you join the crows?"

Karl pauses as though taking stock of me, deciding how much to say.

"I've learned a few things about loyalty. From you, mostly." I look at him, surprised. "You've always done the right thing, even when it meant you suffered. It got me thinking. I used to just want to have an easy life – make money, be successful – but then I realized it wasn't really worth anything if I didn't have a conscience." He carries on walking and I follow.

Karl has brought me through a tucked-away, abandoned corridor to a room that was perhaps once an office, but now acts as a graveyard for broken chairs and tables. I pick my way through piled-up furniture and broken chair legs.

"I'm going to have to lock you up – I need to make it

look like I hauled you in. He has to believe that I'm on his side. I will bring Minnow, saying I've found his murderer. But don't worry, I won't leave you with him."

"No, wait outside," I say. "I want this to just be me and him."

Karl nods his understanding. The door is shut, the lock clicks and I wait, secret in hand, ready to open fire.

Jack Minnow keeps me waiting. I have been standing long enough to wish that just one of these chairs was intact. So, when the door creaks open, it makes me jump. Minnow wanders in, wide contented smile, shoulders back and a swagger in his walk. He didn't think it would be quite this easy.

"Got yourself caught?" He smirks. "Not as clever as you think, are you, Flint?" Minnow flexes his fingers. There is a predatory snarl about him that makes my skin crawl. "The mayor will be thrilled – everything's falling into place." He steps closer and I force myself to stand my ground. I clear my throat.

"Perhaps it's not me who is caught." My voice shakes. "Did you think I had forgotten about you, Minnow?"

His mouth twitches. "Bravado doesn't look good on you. Fearful, cowardly – that's the real you."

I hate that he sees through me, that he seems to know my weaknesses and hopes – he always finds the perfect way to work his way in and shatter them. Not this time.

"You're not going to arrest me," I tell him. "And you're not going to tell Longsight that I was here. I want you to tell me what you've done with Mel. And I want to know where Gull is."

At this, Jack Minnow laughs. Shaking his head, he speaks.

"I assume there is an 'or else. . .' at the end of that impressive list of demands?" His voice is bored.

"Have you forgotten?" It's my turn to smile. "I know about you, Minnow. I know all about your life. You have a secret, and unless you do the things I ask, your secret will be revealed to the world. How do you think the people will react when they hear that your father was a traitor – that he stole from the marked to give to the blanks? What do you think they will do when they discover that you violated our holy place by saying his name over and over, every night? The son of a forgotten daring to defile our community with your wicked words. How will they react, Minnow? What will they do when they discover your sins?"

Minnow looks away, down at the ground. His jaw clenches and I wonder if he will attempt to strike me. One scream though, and Karl will be at my side.

He runs a hand over his shaven head and fixes his eyes

on me. He turns his face, just slightly, towards the door and I think he will try to run. But instead he calls out, "OK."

The handle moves, and I ready myself to see Karl, but my eyes play tricks.

I blink and shake my head; but they're still there. At the door is Verity and she is not alone.

Gull follows her – tall, graceful, for once owning her height.

I rush towards them. I reach out my hands.

"Verity! Gull!" I cry out.

But they do not open their arms to receive me. They step back. Gull moves her hand and clasps Verity's. And Verity smiles. It is not the smile of a friend or the smile of a sister but the smile of an archer who knows that they can shoot true.

For, now that I am close, I can see.

Here is Gull, but she is not the Gull I know. She wears our traditional dress, which is designed to look like a scanty imitation of a warrior's uniform. A leather breastplate, a soft leather skirt. But more than that – she wears our ink. Gull is marked.

When I left her, the only marks Gull had were the ones she made herself, the clumsy lye marks that burned her skin. But now she is a new person. A person made of ink.

Verity has let the arrow fly; watches as the tip pierces my heart. And still she smiles.

Of all the fears I had for Gull – beatings, torture, even death – none come close to this.

"Gull . . . what have you done?" Words pour out before I can stop them, each one dipped in horror.

"See?" She turns to Verity. "So quick to shift the blame, always ready to lay the guilt at someone else's feet."

"Wh. . . I don't know what you mean?" I implore. I will her to see that it's me; it's her friend – the one who saved her from the water, the one who took her away from the danger in Featherstone. "It's me, Gull. Look at me."

Her ice-blue eyes turn on me then and there is nothing but frost in her gaze.

"I'm looking," she says slowly. "Did you look, Leora?" She cocks her head. "Did you look for me – did you even care? Was it your plan all along to leave me to the dogs?"

"What are you saying?" I whisper. "Gull, they caught me – they took me away. I begged them to tell me where you were."

Gull just stares.

"Why would I trust you, Leora?" she says. "Why would I ever trust you?" I want to cry at hearing her say my name. "You lied," Gull states. I've heard this voice in my dreams – but never this loud, never this sure. "You told me lie after lie and I believed you." My hands are still outstretched, still reaching and hoping to find hers.

"I came here expecting to meet devils. Instead I met an angel." I see her clasping Verity's hand more tightly.

"I... I didn't lie," I mumble – I feel like I am on a boat, the ground swaying beneath me. "Gull, I... You're my friend." It sounds so pathetic, like a child in the playground.

"Don't let her talk to you about friendship." Verity's voice is cold. I watch as her fingers squeeze Gull's. "She betrays everyone she claims to love."

"Verity, *Vetty*, come on." My voice wobbles and I blink tears away. "Can't we talk?" Verity raises an eyebrow.

My tired eyes take in Gull's marks. Reading her comes easily. She has no punishment marks.

Up her right arm are commendations, marks that honour her defection. I see them glow almost gold, although the ink beneath her skin is black. The marks sway and glimmer into bright and glorious vignettes. A picture of her leaving home and stepping free from the forest. A scene that shows her accepting her ink like a child accepts a warm coat. I dread to imagine her back. They will not have allowed her to mark her true family on her back – she will have had to renounce them along with everything she has ever known.

"You lied to me," she says again, and this time I cry out:

"What did I lie to you about?"

"You told me horror stories about Saintstone," she says quietly. There is a complacent tone in her voice, a certainty. *This doesn't sound like Gull*, I think. "You told me you were a victim. You said you had been forced to live under a cruel and restrictive regime. You challenged my beliefs, and for that, perhaps I should thank you." I recognize her tone now; she sounds like Longsight. "For I know now that the life I ran from was as false and oppressive as you always said."

As I always said? I'm dizzy, my thoughts make my mind murky and blurred and I feel a tightening of my stomach – a nausea so bitter.

"You never loved Featherstone, but you told me that Saintstone was as bad, if not worse. You told me all your sorry little tales. You made me believe in the ghosts that only you could see." Gull drops Verity's hand gently and runs her fingers down her skirt as though brushing out creases.

My gaze follows, and I see that she has been inked there too – in white. Her legs are like snowflakes – laced with white lines. Her story swims to the surface: a story of a girl who was lost and who has been found. "You brought me here, from everything I knew and believed, and then you left me – abandoned me. You're good at that, aren't you? It was Verity who found me." She holds her hand again.

"I never wanted to leave you," I said.

"And yet. . ." She scowls. "You are only happy when

you're tearing something down. You made me believe that my home was a lie, and that Saintstone was worse. Verity came and reached out her hand and took me with her. I have learned so much. At last, Leora, I have seen the light."

Her scars still cover her arm. I meant them to be like a constellation of stars, a universe beyond. But it looks like the remnants of a sickness – one she was lucky to survive.

There is nothing to say or do.

There is nothing they won't take from me.

Jack Minnow lets the silence bloom into a cloud of poisonous gas, all the time relishing my every breath – gloating over the death of a soul.

"That's what you wanted, yes, Flint?" His voice makes my skin shiver. "I've given you your wish and shown you your ... friend." He drops that word like a burning coal into my hands. "Did you really think you could wield even an ounce of power over me? Threatening to tell my secrets." His mocking voice is on the edge of laughter. "Leora, I have so many secrets. I keep them close and I nurture them. I'm master of my secrets – don't you think by now that I have learned to make my past work for me? As if, by one fell swoop, you could ruin me: you couldn't even make me stumble."

"But if the people knew. . ." I say in a voice so weak it barely carries.

"If the people knew, so what?" he says. "When you have power, even your secrets are assets. Nothing you say can scare or control me. You are nothing – you aren't even worth the hunt." He stands aside, leaving my route to the door clear. "Go, Leora – leave. I have more in store for you; it would be a shame to capture you so quickly."

I begin to walk. When I am almost past him, he calls out, "Catch," and I put out a hand and clutch at what he has thrown.

Opening my hand, I see a small bottle – a familiar shape. A bottle of red ink. I study the label – it's a brand I don't know. My eyes meet Minnow's and he gives a lazy smirk.

"A new kind of ink. Great technological advances."

I examine the bottle again, frowning.

"Imagine an ink made to degrade, ink that is designed to be broken down by the body. The tattoos from ink like this would vanish over a matter of days. It would seem... Well, it would seem almost like a miracle."

I look from the bottle, to Minnow's face.

"The mayor's marks?" I say. My voice is numb.

"You see, Flint. I am not afraid of you knowing my secrets. After all, who would believe you?"

As I run from the room, all I hear is Jack Minnow's laugh echoing in my ears.

Chapter Thirty-five

Once I am outside I see that there is another meeting gathering. Covering my face, I join the throng. It smells of sweat, the inevitable miasma created by a crowd of hot and anxious people stuck in one place. A trickle of perspiration makes its way down my back.

You can see that people are frustrated – reluctant to be here, tired of having their routines constantly upset by public showdowns. The people want action; they want to know how Longsight is going to stop the attacks.

When did it all change? He used to draw respect; there was only silence and awe when he stood before us. How can it be that after everything – his astonishing revival, his incredible feats – he is less impressive? Everything that was once so glittering now seems tarnished. How is it that power can be so easily lost? Fear is a potent brew, and Sana has been letting it simmer to perfection.

I am still stunned from my face-off with Minnow. My fingers brush the bottle of ink in my pocket. All my muscles are tight – as though I've been running or readying myself for a fight. Adrenaline zings around my body, heightening my senses.

When Mayor Longsight takes to the stage – arms outstretched, ready to embrace applause – there is absolute silence.

"My people," he says, and I think his voice falters. "My people, I have heard your cries. You are afraid, and you are hurting. Believe me, I feel your pain in my very core. You wonder why the blanks seem to have grown strong and you ask why we do not show them that we are so much stronger."

There are calls of agreement here, and to my ears they sound irritable. Longsight pauses and inclines his head as though studying the crowd – planning carefully what he will tell them next. I can feel their longing like a current – their fists are clenched, their feet firmly set. They want him to call for them to fight: they have never been so ready. I prepare for him to call out, to raise his voice and rally his troops. Instead he smiles.

"We are at the cusp of something new, something great," Longsight says, and his voice is gaining in confidence. "Have you ever watched someone die?"

That catches their attention. The smile is still playing at his lips and I take an uneasy glance around.

"The death of some*one*, or some*thing* . . . it matters not.

If you have seen death, you may be familiar with what are known as 'death throes'."

I shiver. I'm back in our little house, watching Dad, as Mum holds his hand. I've seen death.

"The death throes are the last attempts of a human or beast to snatch back life. The body jerks, the breath catches, the fingers claw, the rasp of final agony." And still he smiles. "Death throes can look for all the world like life – like a fight that just might be won – they are violent and have a kind of unworldly strength. If you see a person in the throes of death for the first time, you would be forgiven for believing that they are recovering. But those accustomed to death see these exertions for what they are: a clear sign that the end is moments away." He's got the people's attention fully now – all eyes are on him, no one speaks, nobody even shifts their feet or coughs.

"Do not let the blanks fool you, friends." Mayor Longsight places his palm on his chest, as though he is paying us honour. "Their actions: stealing our skin books. Desecrating the sacred hall of remembrance. They are nothing but the frantic final grasps of a people who know their time has come. I admit, death throes are not pleasant to watch – some even find them frightening – but we should not fear these last desperate acts of a frail and useless people. They are dying. All we must do is wait."

Wait? I think. That is the last thing these people desire.

And indeed, there is a low, angry murmur of dissent. He holds out his hands.

"I want us to keep our focus. The people of Saintstone aren't here to fight; we are here to live in peace and prosperity. Let me tell you a story." Someone jeers; they are sick of stories. He ignores them and continues. "I remember our beloved storyteller, Mel, telling me once that she saw a future where there was unity. She saw a time when the blanks would return to us on their knees and beg forgiveness. She predicted a day when all blanks would repent of their obstinate rebellion and see the light. She saw, in her prophetic wisdom, throngs of those who were once blank, willingly coming to purge their sin and be inked. I believe I owe it to her to pursue that vision – we have the truth in our hands, we have the way of salvation on our skin. I am here today to tell you that a renaissance is coming; indeed, that it has already begun."

And I know then what he is planning to do.

"Friends! Today I introduce you to ... the future!" He speaks with a flourish and looks off-stage with an exhilarated expression on his face. I move even closer. The people are still quiet.

Verity leads the way and behind her comes Gull, shrouded in cloth. Her shy, hopeful smile brings tears to my eyes. If I can just get near enough—

This isn't going to work. Longsight has misjudged the crowd. Please, no.

"Many of you will remember the day Leora Flint returned to us – that traitor, still missing, still a threat to our peace." I look around, waiting for someone to notice me and call me out. "However, you may not know that another young woman arrived in our midst that day. And, although with the return of Flint came a resurgence of darkness, there was a little light. Of course, initially we were uncertain – for the one who came to our town with Leora Flint was blank."

Voices rumble around me. It feels like distant thunder before the storm breaks. *No*, the voice in my head whispers. *No. No. No.*

But she's there. They're both standing right there – a proud and faithful Verity and a brave, foolish Gull – skin hidden for now, safe only because of the fabric wrapped around her.

Longsight keeps talking.

"I am here to tell you that Mel was right – there is hope, and that hope can be found in unity. That the blanks will return, return to the land and the culture they shunned; and when they come they will kneel and they will beg to be brought into the way of truth."

"And we'll destroy them!" one lone voice hollers.

Mayor Longsight pauses, head cocked. He takes a breath. I am almost at the stage.

"We will not destroy them, no." He's quieter now and all the more sinister for it. "We will *test* them." There is a pause and he looks around. "Why has all this happened, now? My resurrection, my body becoming immortal? Because now is a new beginning. It is time for the blanks to call upon us for mercy and submit to the truth – confessing their evil ways and undergoing the inker's needle. And then we will bring them in. A new, united community – the lost souls found."

It is as though he is impervious to the simmering rage and disbelief that froths through the crowd. The heat has been turned up – it is unbearable, oppressive. Faces that are damp with perspiration are ready to bay for the cooling rain of blood. And yet, Longsight takes the quiet as assent, as support – and he unveils his masterpiece.

Gull removes her cloak.

The chatter begins from the people farthest away from the stage. It is hard for them to see white on white – the cobweb delicacy of the ink on Gull's pale skin. Their questions ebb forward and the answer flows back: "The blank is marked." The roar hits as my foot strikes the stage. The people aren't impressed – they see a blank in inked clothing, an imposter, blasphemy personified.

And they will not stand for it. They surge to the stage, trampling those who move too slowly. A guard moves to prevent them using the steps, but he is punched mercilessly and falls under their feet. I have barely a second. I rush forward, barge Longsight out of my way and take the microphone off its stand. I am the only help that is going to come.

"People of Saintstone!" I speak into the microphone but am not heard above the chaos. I yell. "People of Saintstone, stop and look at me!" It is like watching dominoes fall as one person sees who it is that addresses them and alerts their neighbour – the buzz passes through until all the focus is on me, the crowd still screaming in thirsty rage.

"Do not be hasty. Do not behave in a way that would shame your ancestors." I'm having to scream every word. "Whatever you do today will be on your conscience and in your soul for ever."

Sensing a tiny shift in the tension of the crowd, I risk a glance over my shoulder. The people who were storming the stage are held back for now. Gull looks bewildered and her eyes meet mine, silent, screaming terror. I see a glimpse of the friend she was – the friend who was always afraid, the one who always wanted to get it right and yet even her own people called her a curse. She stands here rejected again. She's followed the rules, she's got it right – done her best – but it is not enough.

More guards pour into the square from the government building and now that the crowd is under control their focus switches – to me.

I unwind the shawl that covers my face.

"I am Leora Flint. Your traitor, your fugitive." The guards on the stage edge closer, like dogs being told to wait by their master. Mayor Longsight looks on, his bafflement turned to delight, gloating and gratified that he has smoked me out. "I don't ask for you to believe me – I only beg that you hear me." A shift behind me; a guard is distracted. "I am not here to ruin you or betray you – I am here for the truth. The truth is that you cannot trust those who lead you. You are being lied to every day. The mayor's marks that disappeared, his resurrection – they are a lie!"

And that's when they pounce. It feels like ten, twenty guards have all descended as one to subdue me – as though I am a bear, a wolf, a witch. The microphone slams on to the ground, the percussive blow cracks through the speakers like a slaying. My head is held against the wood of the staging platform, and between legs and clomping feet, I see something that gives me one tiny beacon of hope.

Gull and Verity are gone.

Chapter Thirty-six

So much for being in control of my own life. Sitting in a prison cell with only a mattress and a bucket for company doesn't feel much like autonomy. But if this is what it takes to keep my friends safe, then I would do it again and again.

I am in a cell next door to Connor's, with Obel diagonally opposite me and, as I sit cross-legged with my forehead resting heavily on the bars, he starts to talk.

"I've not been a good man, Leora." I don't look his way, just let his words come like the buzz of a fly trapped inside. "When I came to Saintstone I thought I saw my chance to be free. Here was this town where I could fulfil my dream of being an inker – I achieved my greatest ambition the day I opened the studio. But every day I was terrified." I lift my eyes at this. "All it would take was one person discovering my secret and everything I'd worked so hard for – everything I had earned – it all would have been lost. I thought I'd found a place I belonged, but the only way I could live was by lying every day. When I was trying to be the real me, it meant I didn't belong in Featherstone, and when I found a place that felt like home, the only way I could be safe was by covering up the real me in paint and lies. A precarious state, but I thought it was freedom. I heard the news coming from Featherstone. I knew what was happening – the suffering and misery – but I couldn't stand up for them without risking all that I'd worked for. So, when I met you, I saw an answer."

"Oh don't, Obel. I can't listen to another talk about me being the special one. Look where it's got me."

"That's the thing, girl. I didn't think you were special, not at first. But I thought that if I could make you believe you were – if I convinced you and pushed you – then maybe you could do the work that I was too afraid to do. You, the perfect candidate: a blank in marked skin, a marked with blank blood. Who better to send a message of hope to Featherstone and to fight for their freedom? I told myself it was true. I didn't lie – I just controlled some of the ways you found out your story. I told myself that for the sake of my family at home, it was OK – that this is what your dad would have wanted anyway. But it wasn't my story to tell. I should never have pushed you the way I did. I made you go to Featherstone, when really, I knew the responsibility lay with me – it should have been me going back to help my people. I manipulated you and I knew I was doing it."

Was it manipulation, I wonder? All I wanted was to please my teacher and become good at the job. It didn't feel anything like coercion – it felt like I was special: finally, *finally* in the role I had yearned for and feeling like I was in a secret club. And then, knowing he trusted me – enough to let me in on his secrets and mine. Well, it just felt good.

"I let you take risks that should never have been yours to take. I was a coward – and I still am. But, girl, you did everyone proud. You're the bravest person I know."

The bars press against my brow like an iron headache, but still I don't move. *I could sleep here*, I think. *I could die here.*

In my dream I walk hand in hand with Mel. Each step with her brings me strength. As we walk, she tells a story.

They say that gods do not sleep. For, if they did, the world would have to stop and wait until they woke. All these small moments that you rely on, the magic of breath and heartbeat – the things that must keep on and keep on lest you die, they are only possible because you have gods who do not slumber.

A god beneath a blanket, eyes closed and passive – well, that god could be crept up on; that god could be killed in their sleep. For sleep is a vulnerable state and one does not creep up on a god. A god must not die.

A princess may sleep. She may sleep for one hundred years if she so wishes. But while she sleeps she cannot play or charm or rule. No wonder sleep is a curse used by witches. While the princess sleeps the witch can play and charm and rule in their place.

What should you do if you see a sleeping princess? Oh, you will pause awhile and watch — they rest their hands so nicely, their hair fans out so prettily, their lips look their most kissable. Aren't they lovely when they're asleep? But while they sleep their lands are going to ruin; while they sleep their people are being slaughtered; while they sleep evil can walk freely.

We must wake them, but how?

With a kiss? Don't be creepy.

With a shake? Perhaps that might work.

With a slap? I'm afraid we can't.

Let us shout, let us call out in our loudest voices:

WAKE UP.

Wake up, princesses and see the destruction.

Wake up, princesses and see that while you have had your eyes shut, every terrible thing has crept into your world.

Wake up, princesses. WAKE UP.

When they wake they will weep. But then they will act.

A princess cannot sleep for ever.

Chapter Thirty-seven

I have been given traditional clothes to wear. A pleated leather skirt and breastplate. It shows every tattoo that I bear on my skin – including the mark that has appeared most recently; the mark of the reunited sisters, their hands clasped, is front and centre. It is a grim walk with guards either side of me and Minnow heading up our procession, and my skin is covered with goosebumps of fear. I have been allowed to wear my own boots and they pad gently as we head towards the hall of judgement.

We enter through a side door, and it's a good thing, because there is a queue from the main doors that almost fills the square. The hall is big, but not big enough to contain the entire community – perhaps it was once. But that doesn't seem to have stopped the whole of Saintstone trying to come and get a glimpse of what Mayor Longsight has planned for that treacherous, deceiving, murderous Leora Flint.

The last time I was here, my life changed for ever. I

found out all my secrets, the secrets that so many people seemed to already know. All the hatred I'd been taught to feel for the blanks – all the fear too – meant that I gave up on my own father that day.

I had only ever seen one half of the world. As far as I knew, the earth was flat. It took going to the other side, exchanging my ignorance for experience, before I could see the perfect beauty of the full globe. It gleams in my memory now, like a crystal ball, but I'm no longer asking it what my future holds. I just want to show everyone its splendour.

I am made to stand on the dais, there for all the people to gaze upon while they wait for the show to begin. A while after I arrive. Obel and Connor are brought on to the platform too – I don't know why – and they stand at the back. Mayor Longsight sits upon an ornately carved wooden chair. Minnow is behind him, alert and watchful. Longsight is enjoying the thrum of excitement that is building around us.

I refuse to keep my eyes down. I'm not here to be cowed or scared; I'm not going to behave as though I am guilty and ashamed. I stare into the eyes of every person sitting in row after row, until they are so high and so far above me I cannot make out their features. It's the missing people I notice first – no Gull or Verity – although I can see Simon and Julia, Verity's parents, and Seb sitting with them. He waves and my facade almost crumbles.

Mum is here. I see her face and I nearly cry out – I know the courage it has taken for her to even leave the house. She is sitting near the front, where she can't see the stares from the people behind her. She has chosen to sit where I can see her, and when I look at her, all I see is love. It pulses from her, almost pounding at my heart. Her eyes, her face – that small, strong smile, the merest nod of support that feels like stadia of cheers. She is not broken; she is not crushed. I have never seen a human so strong, so noble, so beautiful as my mother at that moment. I keep my eyes on her and nothing else touches me because her love is a mountain, her love is armour, her love is a shield that cannot be destroyed.

When Jack Minnow steps forward, a hush inhales around the hall. Was this what he meant, when he said he had more in store for me?

He calls for silence with none of Longsight's flourishes. When he speaks his voice is matter of fact and calm, but all the more impressive for it.

"Thank you for coming. Today is a day for justice: justice and celebration. I have been given permission to speak on our great leader's behalf; it is thanks to him that this enemy of our custom – this terrible threat to our commonality – has been brought to be reckoned."

I don't know whether it's because it's Minnow saying it, or because the people finally have someone to unite them in hate, but Jack Minnow's words are falling on willing ears. There is a murmur of warmth and support.

"And so, it is my honour to present to you our own Mayor Dan Longsight, whose wisdom and faithfulness is unsurpassed."

There is some applause. Not quite the powerful adulation of his glory days, but applause nonetheless. How quickly people's allegiances change. Now I realize that Longsight must live his life in fear of those changes in taste and favour.

Mayor Longsight rises and steps forward. He has only a covering tied at his waist: no gown this time, he is just skin and ink and scar. His ink – oh, his ink is too beautiful for one so crazed with hate. He is covered in the most complex marks: geometry and angles – lines and shapes that speak of sacred numbers, the mysteries of the universe, infinity and abundance. But today I see them dance in skeletal staccato – smooth sides and tight angles look to me like the sharpest of blades. He radiates assurance.

When he speaks, it is brief. "According to our customs and laws, I judge that Leora be marked with the crow and forgotten for ever."

My reaction is almost one of disappointment. It is very nearly an anti-climax. And yet, the response from the people gratifies Mayor Longsight. This is still a relatively seldom seen and shocking punishment.

I know with certainty then that I don't believe any more. I remember Connor Drew's marking, and my unshakeable belief that his soul was being destroyed. We all saw it that way – that his one route to salvation, the only means by which he would be remembered and live eternally, had been cut off. A skin book would be made, but it would be destroyed by the fire of judgement. I saw a man without hope, without any future or purpose in living. I saw in him my own father who, according to our customs, also deserved nothing more than to be instantly forgotten by all at his death. The horror of it grabbed my throat; it kept me awake; it motivated everything – I had to save my father.

And yet here I am, about to marked with a crow. And I feel no terror at eternal damnation. The onlookers may be feeling all that I did on that strange day in the autumn of last year, but I feel impermeable. Shave my hair, mark me with ink – my soul remains.

What hurts is that it's Obel who will do it.

He pushes me down so that I kneel before the crowd. His hand presses my head forward and I hear the rasp of scissors cutting away a handful of hair at the back of my head. *It must be hurting his hand*, I think. A block is brought for me to rest my head on as he trims more hair and then shaves the patch clean with a razor. I feel his warm hands on my scalp, the stroke of the blade, the tickle of hair being brushed away. His hands feel steady, even though I know the impossible act of will it must take for him to not cry out in pain as he wields tools in his right hand. The mark won't be pretty; I know that much.

I wish I didn't love that sound – the buzz of the machine, the way the note changes when the needle hits skin, the melody of it bouncing around my skull while Obel draws with ink, letting it ram a million times into my flesh. Every time he lifts the machine to dip into ink I feel relief and then he plunges once more. The pain is like bites – the beaky pecks of a crow.

When I stand up, dizzy and sweating, to face the crowd it seems like a held breath is released and the people get to their feet, stamping so hard the room quakes. They clap, they cheer, they jeer – making faces and grim gestures just for me. In this moment, everything they have hated, all the ways they have been mistreated and misled, are thrown at me in a crazed catharsis of screams and wails of celebration.

What happens now? I risk a glance towards Mayor Longsight and, although he is applauding too, I can tell – or sense – he is not finished with me. The fire burns on, and so does his vengeance.

I do the only thing that gives me power, and let my remaining hair fall about my shoulders, allowing my ink to be hidden. Mum used to tell me to keep my head down, but when I look her way, I know that neither of us believe that any more. We both stand tall, shoulders strong and feet planted. We are not meant to bow like snowdrops – heads hanging drooped; we are ancient trees – strong as oak.

And so, I barely notice as two people bring on a new contraption. The audience sees though, and the yells peter out. A hushed silence falls.

A small square of the platform – about the size of my spread-out hand – is pulled up by an inset ring and flipped on its hinge. Into it is thrust a wooden T-shaped frame, just a little less tall than I am. I wish I hadn't been thinking about trees because now this reminds me of one – the roughness of the wood, the knots and grain showing through. It leans back at about seventy-five degrees and instead of leaves or bark, there are leather straps. My lungs have shrunk, I think – I can't take in proper breaths; someone has them squeezed in their hands.

Mayor Longsight steps forward once again and I am a creature stunned by fear. Jack Minnow comes up behind me and pins my wrists in his hands. I pull with all my strength, trying to break from his grip. But he's always been stronger. The mayor addresses his people.

"I take great joy in your loyalty as you celebrate with me the marking of a forgotten. But doesn't this feel just a little like a sentence that has no full stop? Aren't we missing something of the satisfaction of seeing *full* justice be done?" He looks around the room at faces that hold frozen half-smiles, cheers still fresh on their lips – but there is a new tension that hisses in the gaps.

"We are here this morning for justice. And justice is what you will get."

Minnow pulls me aside then, and my heels push against the base of the wooden T. Leather straps are pulled tightly and buckled by assistants while Jack Minnow keeps hold of my wrists and smirks his delight at me. At last, he has me where he wants me. They have won. He lifts one of my arms and binds it to the crosspiece. My chest is stretched by the reach it forces, and pain sings through my shoulders as my other wrist is bound too. The angle of the frame means I have to lean back as though I am at the beginning of a fall. They made us do trust exercises when we were at school; I only ever trusted Verity enough to fall back and believe she would catch me. The wood creaks but holds me; my chest rises and falls – each breath an effort of will and strength. I can feel the soles of my soft boots beginning to slip forward and the movement makes me hang lower, leather biting into my wrists.

"Of course, we abide by our own rules – she must have a skin book, she must have her mark of the forgotten read, and her skin book must be burned in the fire of judgement." It's hard to see anyone with my head thrown back and it hurts to lift it, but I hear the rumbles of conversation that travel through the rows of people.

"For a skin book to be produced," Longsight continues, "the body must be flayed."

Voices rise in a bustle of shock and confusion. My insides freeze and shatter. I have tried to be brave, I have tried to be strong and good, but there's nothing left. I can hear my mum's voice screaming and my torso shakes in sobs, heaving against my pinioned arms. I gasp in air and hold it, telling myself I only need to hold on a little longer. I will not let them win; I can't let them break me – even if they take my skin, they will not take my honour. I clench my teeth – they will not hear me scream.

In my peripheral vision a figure to my right steps forward. The light from the fire catches on something in his hand and a metallic flash sears my eyes. I blink and look again. I know those marks – it is Connor. It's a final blow that the man who tried to save my father is being made to destroy me.

Longsight's voice rings out. "As your leader and your judge, it falls to me – this great honour – to be the one to make the first incision."

I hear someone in the first row cry out, "No!" I hear voices raised in surprise and horror. This isn't what the crowd want, I think; he has misjudged things yet again. And as the knife is passed to Mayor Longsight I hear my mum calling out to me in a voice desperate and pure, "Be strong, my little light." But skin is not strong – if it were we would not be able to force ink beneath its surface; our hairs would not raise in delight at the touch of a person we've longed for; we would not laugh when tickled or cry when bruised. Here I am with my skin on display, throat bare, stomach vulnerable. My skin will be cut and peeled from me like it was from Saint, but I will not weep with joy at the releasing of my soul. I will only bleed.

Chapter Thirty-eight

Connor Drew is coaching the mayor quietly, so only I can hear.

"A shallow cut, or the skin will be tainted and void. A steady hand, yes. Do you see here where the skin beneath the breastplate is very smooth? It requires a cut that just barely curves upward, like a smile." I feel him trace a line on my body with his fingernail and my breath shudders. "Follow that course, or the tanning will not be true, and the edges will have to be trimmed."

He sounds like Obel when he taught me about ink and marks, the calm focus of a master at work.

"Connor," I whimper, and his eyes meet mine. "Don't do this. Help me." He could save me. He could do something. He wouldn't collude with Longsight, not after everything he's fought for.

There is a storm of sadness behind his eyes and I can see nothing of Oscar's bright, fierce loyalty. Connor drops his gaze with a shake of his head.

"It's him or you," Longsight jeers. "And who would die in your place?"

Hope drops me then, and Connor clears his throat, ready to continue his gruesome patter.

"One cut, Mayor Longsight, and then I take over – this is painstaking work; it must be done right."

I see the mayor raise the knife aloft. The crowd is noisy, and I hear people from outside pressing at the doors wanting to come and see. The mayor straddles the frame and looks into my face. A bold girl would spit, a brave person would speak. I am neither. He holds me at my neck, pressing down enough for my breath to catch. I wriggle and shift, trying to move my body away, but he just nods to Minnow, who cracks me across the cheek. I don't know if it's tears or blood or sweat that drips from my face, but I am done. It starts with a cut, Dad used to tell me, and then the gentle easing away of skin from flesh.

Pushing my chin up and resting his forearm on my chest Longsight's panting is in my ear; his spit curdles at the corner of his mouth and his eyes are alight – brighter and more terrible than the fire behind him.

"One cut," he whispers. "I'll be sure to make it last." Biting his lip, breath quivering, he focuses on my skin.

Some people say that when a cut is clean the pain doesn't register. If that is so, then this was no clean cut.

Sometimes pain can sing, it rings so pure. Other times

it screams raggedly. But this pain, oh this pain is a wail. The point of the knife punctures the skin like the wail of a mother whose baby is being wrenched from her arms. The edge draws against the skin like the wail of a mourner. The blade drags and sinks like the wail of a creature caught in a trap. The incision gapes like the wail of families torn apart. The knife lifts like the wail of a child for whom no one will come.

But I don't cry out – for this is just the start.

Through tears, I see the blur of a bloodied knife being passed back to Connor, and I brace my sweat-slicked back against the post, readying myself for the greater pain to come. He stands as Longsight had, feet either side of my own, but his hand rest on my arm, not my throat.

In a tone that reminds me too much of Oscar, he murmurs, "I'm sorry," and I squeeze my eyes shut, praying that I might pass out quickly rather than experience hours of this agony. I blink, and the knife is raised once again. He brings it down fast – too fast – and my arm falls free. He leans and slashes through the leather holding my other wrist and then turns, stance bold, muscles tensed, ready to fight.

Chapter Thirty-nine

It takes me a moment to understand, to see. I nearly faint from pain when I bend to unbuckle the straps at my ankles. But after a minute, I stand – free. Bloody and broken, but free. Obel has the mayor pinned to the ground – none of the guards come to help him – and Connor – well, you don't hand a knife to a criminal. Connor looms over Longsight, the bloodied blade at his throat.

I wait for the crowd to descend. But the people aren't coming to their leader's aid. They look astonished, but not angry. I glance around, but I see no sign of Jack Minnow. I wish I was a snake and I could taste the air to get a flavour of the atmosphere. Instead I pause and watch and listen until I'm sure, and it's ... relief. The overriding mood is cautious, shocked relief.

I am surprised to see my own mother on the platform, standing central. She has a bag over her shoulder and she looks so small.

"Were you all planning to watch?" my mother's voice

echoes around the room. "We are a community who pride ourselves on our goodness, who declare it daily on our skin, and we are a people proud enough to enter eternity with bravado. But you would sit comfortably and watch a child be slaughtered? Oh, you weren't holding the knife – but if you watch and do not shout 'Stop', you are sanctioning everything you see. You were sanctioning the slaughter of a child: my child. What were you afraid of? Why did not you call out your horror at what your leader was attempting to do? Had he succeeded, it would have been a sin forever etched upon your soul. But no, you are good people. You would have comforted yourself with that. Whereas these sinners in your midst, these so-called criminals," she gestures to Obel and Connor, "were willing to stand and fight. They have saved you from blood-guilt and they have saved my girl, my Leora." I think she will cry, but she puts her palm on her chest and controls herself. "I knew a man once who told me that what matters most is the life we live and not our death. The man who taught me all these things was my husband and Leora's father. He was a forgotten and he is dead now. He did not want a skin book made, but I begged him to and he agreed. I was so afraid – afraid of life without him and scared of what being forgotten truly meant." Mum reaches into her bag and pulls out Dad's skin book. "This is not him, not truly." She lifts his book. "But if he were here today he would be shocked to see that our divisions have only deepened; he would be astonished at the slavish way you follow your leaders. He would call out your preoccupation with the dead. We must now consider the living – and I include all the living when I say this, no matter what their skin says about their choices. We must consider the living and we ourselves must choose life."

This is nothing like the quiet earlier – this is a quiet of peace, of holiness, of knowing that right here a sacred thing has occurred. It is in this beautiful silence that my mum steps forward and kisses my dad's book.

And then she throws it into the fire.

Chapter Forty

In spite of my protests, Mum allows Verity's father, Simon, to come with us back to house. I lie on my bed while he cleans and stitches the slice across my torso. He's a skin specialist and tells me the cut's not deep. His words are meant to comfort, but I can still feel Longsight's touch on me. While Simon works he describes his shock – he had no idea what the mayor had planned, he says. But he flushes with shame when I ask him about the mayor's miraculous new ink. Is there anyone who wasn't caught up in this?

When Simon is gone I put on all the clothes I can find. I can't stop shivering and I cannot bear to have my skin on show. I feel dirty: from the prison, from the smoke smell in my hair, from the sweat and the blood and the hands – all the hands on me without permission – and finally, I sleep.

Whatever hope I had that the people would rise up and claim their own right to rule is quashed by morning. Mum wakes me with tea and the news that Jack Minnow has issued a statement. Those who heard his announcement at the town square first thing this morning were given letters – printed copies of his words to pass on to their neighbours. Mum lets me read.

> *My fellow citizens,*
>
> *I have written these words a hundred times in my mind and it is something of a relief to finally be able to put my thoughts on paper. The last months have been the hardest and most upsetting in our history.*
>
> *Since I was a young man I have followed and supported Dan Longsight. I looked up to him, and the day I was made his advisor was the proudest of my life. Not only was he, in my mind, a wonderful and inspiring leader, he was a man I considered a friend – even a brother.*
>
> *The pain you feel today is an echo of the heartbreak I have experienced, having to witness the downfall of the man I most admired and, hardest of all, having to keep the truth from you, my own community.*
>
> *Looking back, perhaps I should have seen it sooner, but what I now know to have been delusions of grandeur, I believed was simply the confidence of a*

great man. He would tell me he believed himself to be immortal and I believed in his purity of heart as surely as I saw the ink on his skin.

I am ashamed to admit that I helped him. I can only wonder that perhaps I was so willing to trust him, I didn't listen to my own conscience. I have learned that lesson in the most painful ways possible. Intelligence had come telling us that the blanks intended to find an opportunity to assassinate the mayor, and I confess, I aided him in manipulating our enemy to play into our hands. We fed the blanks information; we knew they were coming – we had practically invited them. We worked to orchestrate the entire thing. The waistcoat Mayor Longsight wore that day had an inner lining that protected his body from the full force of blade – his was only a surface wound. In his pockets were pouches of blood. The mayor had commanded me, and I obeyed. I let you believe he had died. For that I am truly sorry. But our deception didn't stop there. During the times you came to see his body in state your mayor was merely sedated.

You may ask why I agreed to be part of this, but to that I can only say, you knew him too – don't you remember how easy it was to be tied up by his words? I would have followed him to the ends of the earth. The truth is, I still trusted him – I believed he had a good plan and that I would see its meaning as it unfolded.

Of course, I had not prepared myself for his illness. That is the only way I can describe it – an illness – as though his mind was taken and his sense all but gone. I wept when I realized that something had changed in him – that at some point when he was playing dead for the crowds, he began to believe his own lie.

The doctor I consulted was sworn to secrecy – I could not bear for you to know that this great man had been so utterly broken. The doctor recommended that I play along – he felt that disagreement and conflict would only harm the mayor's mind even more. Dan Longsight's only hope for healing, the physician told me, lay in my allowing his delusions to play out. We hoped it would cause everything to click back into place once he saw his own madness for what it was.

His marks were fabricated, a miracle staged, and yet still he didn't see reason. He stole a blank, allowed her into our town. He had her marked, believed he could change the truths we have always trusted in. He thought he was authority enough to decide her fate.

He refused to let me enact our revenge on the blanks for their heinous attacks and he heard your hurt and rage. He did not think it necessary. He believed he was a god.

Yesterday, he went too far. He tried to flay a young woman, Leora Flint. Those convicts, Obel Whitworth

*and Connor Drew, are heroes for their actions. I held
back the guards who would have stopped them acting.
As a mark of honour to them, they have been freed from
the prison.*

*I assure you that Dan Longsight is in the best of
hands – he is receiving the highest care in a private
section of the hospital. We must pray for his ancestors to
show him mercy.*

*I hope you will see that finally we can stand
together. For I understand your fear and hurt, your
bewildered mourning echoes my own. You are not the
only victims of Dan Longsight's strange reign. I offer my
services to you as an equal. It will be my honour to lead
my community into peace and justice.*

I tear the letter to pieces. There is no justice – the liars
always win. I pull the covers over my head and hide away
from a world that is worse than I ever could have believed.

Chapter Forty-one

Day and night are meaningless. Hours don't matter. Days pass and weeks do too. A relentless cold has got into my bones and all through summer I stay in my room. Mum brings me food and cups of tea. Seb tries to tempt me with cake.

Verity visits me faithfully – she just sits on the bed next to me and holds my hand. Those are the moment I feel the permafrost could melt, but by the time I think I might speak to her, she's gone. Until one day, the silence breaks.

"What happened to us?" Verity sighs. "You were my sister and I let you become my enemy." She takes my hand and squeezes it. "Leora, I was so afraid of you – and afraid of believing you. Because if what you said about the blanks was true then I was living for a lie. And, yes – I see now that it was a lie. Longsight wasn't the good man I wanted him to be, and whatever spell Jack Minnow cast that entranced me has broken. You were right that there was more than I could see and I was too scared to open my eyes."

I can't speak, but her words are balm. Verity touches my bare foot with her own and our tattoos are side by side.

"We got these marks because we wanted to be the same – we wanted to stay together and be entwined." Her seed mark is still bright and clear – the vines she has inked since are flourishing. "But we weren't in control, were we? We couldn't hold the future." With her brown toes she strokes my mark – the egg with its cracked shell – and I reluctantly smile at the tickle, taking a quick glance at her face. Tears stream down her cheeks.

"Just look, Leora. Your mark compared to mine."

The difference is plain to see. My ink is already growing fuzzy at the edges and the colour has faded to grey. The egg looks like it has been broken many times from all the walks through the woods, the barefoot adventures with Gull, the times I had to run or to wade through water – the times I had to scramble away from danger.

"I will never know all you have been through," she says. "I am sorry, Leora. One day, I hope that you might be able to forgive me."

I squeeze her hand. The thaw has begun.

Minnow is leading like he wanted to all along and there is something like peace, for now. I think about Longsight sometimes, and wonder whether he knows that it was his friend Jack who sent him mad. For I don't believe a word of that letter. It was Minnow, all Minnow, I know it. Longsight was just his puppet, a vain man manipulated by a clever one.

I hear snippets of news.

Gull is staying with Verity's family. Penance, I think, for Simon's deceit; because he was the doctor – the one who operated on the mayor, the one who sedated him, the one who let him be marked with ink that vanished in a week. Some days I think he was just foolish, but on others I think of him like a conductor – the small movements of his hands creating whole swells and shrieks of discord. He stayed away from Mum not because he was fearful of her, but because he could not bear to face her.

There is no word of Mel. Karl is trying to solve that mystery, but he has to be careful. I hope that he is being careful.

I know everyone dreams. I like to believe our dreams unite us when nothing else will. It comforts me to think that we all know that feeling when you wake up, and the world feels as though it's shifted or been painted a different shade.

Maybe the dreamer dreams of kissing someone they shouldn't, and for days after, they watch that person when they talk and their heart races at the way their lips caress each word. They had never seen that before.

Or, the dreamer dreams their friend betrayed them, and even though the daylight tells them it was only in their head, they still find they need to forgive them for hurting them, and for ever after the dreamer knows that they could – the seed has been sown and the dreamer believes their friend has it in them to break their heart.

The dreamer dreams and wakes in terror, feeling that the danger has not left with sleep, and they try to tell someone in the hope that they will offer comfort, but instead they look as though the dream has revealed some hidden madness. And the dreamer doesn't know whether it's the dream or the friend's response, but the taste of fear never quite leaves their tongue.

And every dreamer has been the one to hold another and whisper, "It was just a dream." A five-word lie we are all desperate to believe.

Dreams have magic deep within them – and my dreams feel like the most real thing in my life at the moment. And the stories too – they comfort me. I read the final story

Mel received over and over every day, wondering if there's something there that I've missed.

Until, towards the end of the summer Jack Minnow makes a new pronouncement. Mum tells me about it, sitting on my bed.

News has come to Minnow, he says, that the blanks are readying themselves for new attacks. This time, they threaten the one thing our people still have left: their marks.

Minnow has warned people to avoid being marked for the time being. Intelligence says that the blanks intend to poison our ink stores. They have already discovered one tainted batch, and Minnow says that it is indisputably the work of the blanks. Now that I know Jack Minnow likes to play around with people's ink, I don't know if I believe him when he blames Featherstone. I do know that all of this hurts the people of Saintstone horribly. They still have their books in the museum and now they lose access to new ink. Whoever is responsible for the latest ink ban, I have to admit it does have the flavour of one of Sana's plans: her exquisite knack of pressing right where it will hurt the most. The only thing is, in Jack Minnow, Sana finally has an adversary that will fight back as dirtily as she does.

For Minnow has a solution.

He asks the new storyteller, a young man called Noah,

to tell the story of the sisters. Mum says he told it badly; she doesn't like the sound of his voice. At the story's end Minnow comes forward.

"They spread like gangrene, the ways of the blanks. A doctor doesn't treat a patient's gangrene – they chop it out, for they know the only other option is death. Our first leaders knew how to deal with opposition. They were no fools when there was a threat to their way of living. I propose we return to the old ways. The blanks won't leave us alone. They insist on attacking, in spite of our years of patience. They pollute and ooze their evil ways into our lives. No matter. The time has come for us to cut them off. Saintstone . . . beginning tomorrow, we will build a wall."

Brick by brick, my defences rise. There is no point fighting fate – history only repeats, and the winners are all the same.

Chapter Forty-two

I am dropped from the heavens into deep water. A stone that sinks, leaving only a circle of ripples. Although the water is cold, it does not shock me – I am only embraced by a lovely darkness. At the bottom of the water, on the silty ground, are white stones and white bones – skeletal remains of the souls that have been passed over in this place. Lives that were not worth saving, sacrificed for their own good. The claws of a ribcage beckon like loving arms waiting to embrace me, and I plunge deeper still.

I feel the hands of the dead reach out and tug my arms and I gladly submit. Only, the hands pinch my skin with warmth and instead of sinking I feel my body rise up. I want to clutch hold of the grinning skulls beneath me and lay my body on theirs, femur to femur, radius wrapped around rib, metacarpal on spine.

The water wants me: it sucks at me while tugging hands force me along and out. I feel the surface like an umbilical slicing and I cry out, lungs clear.

A baby cries.

I must still be dreaming. I sleep again.

I am held in their arms and wrapped in blankets, brought into their cottage where the fire is lit. One blank, one marked, both with love and concern in their eyes.

They tend to me, feed me, nourish and heal me. The fire melts the ice within me and through the thaw a bud of hope begins to rise.

The sisters coax me back to life with tea and soft singing.

They tell me that I am safe – even when I cry they do not stop saying it. You are safe, you are safe, you are safe.

They show me the candle that has been constantly burning on the table next to where I lie.

"Just a little light," they say, putting a taper to the candle flame, letting it fizz to life.

"Just a little light," they say, taking the taper across to the hearth.

"Just a little light," they say as the kindling singes and smokes.

"Just a little light," they say as the wood crackles and spits.

"But, oh what a great fire a little light can bring."

And the fireplace glows with warmth and bright, dancing fire. And I know I'm ready, although I am just a little light.

Chapter Forty-three

My dream makes me urgent this morning. I emerge on the landing, the first time I have left my room in weeks. I wonder if I am hearing things when a rumble of chatter whips up the stairs. I draw my dressing-gown more tightly round me and step down into a kitchen full of people. Full of blanks.

Oscar catches me when I lose my footing – my body so weak from my time in the cocoon. When he wraps his arms tightly around me and draws me in, my head against his chest, I let myself cry. And I sob for the first time since the day Longsight tried to flay me. I sob for the girl I was who worked so hard, who wanted to be brave and thought that doing the right thing would be enough. I sob for the fractures in all my relationships and for the people I have lost. I still have love for them clinging on to me with nowhere for it to go. I cry too because his strong arms and his warm body remind me of the dream and I weep because I love those sisters who drew me up from the depths and showed me the light.

When I move he lifts my chin and kisses my tear-jewelled eyelashes, making me cry harder still.

Finally, with everyone squeezed into the small space, I ask them their tale. And, although they must have told the story many times, they begin again: Solomon, Tanya, Kasia and Fenn, Penny and Blake and ... a baby.

"Another wall? We could not stand it. We saw marked workers digging out the ancient stones – the original bricks of the wall Moriah called for – and we knew what was happening."

"Why didn't you come sooner? We would have gladly welcomed you." It is Mum.

"It was dangerous." Blake speaks up. I never knew him well in Featherstone, but he was always courageous enough to ask questions and to stand up for what his pregnant wife Penny needed. "We knew the baby could come any day – I refused to take the risk. I didn't want Penny to have to give birth in the middle of the forest with no help, no support." Penny takes up the story.

"Of course, had we realized what would happen, we might have chosen differently." She gives a small smile and her cheeks are pink now that everyone is looking her way. "Sky was born in the evening, during the community fireside time." She pauses to let her words sink in but when she sees confusion on Mum's face, Penny explains. "According to tradition, a baby who is born during the fireside meeting is destined to be either a great blessing, or. . ." she swallows. "A curse."

"No prizes for guessing what Sana's conclusion was." Fenn's voice is gruff, and I can tell from his eyes that he has seen too much – being a spy and acting as one of Sana's closest followers has scarred him. "There was no doubt in her mind. Because you had the gall to challenge her from time to time, she declared immediately that you were the source of another curse." He looks grim. "There was nothing else for us to do but run."

Penny reaches out to him, puts her hand over his. "You saved us, Fenn. You are a good man and so brave." Tears spill from her eyes and Tanya buries her head in her hands. Solomon is not ashamed of his tears and the look in his eyes is one of utmost pride and admiration.

Kasia continues the story.

"Those of us who could no longer bear Sana's rule fled too. Although Sana and her companions despise the marked for beginning to rebuild the wall, their solution is simply to fight more, shed blood and scream all the louder. They have no sorrow at the deepening of division between our communities. We know that coming to Saintstone is foolish – we don't expect to stay – but we could not stay in Featherstone any longer."

Oscar leans into me, lips tickling my neck. No one else can hear him whisper just to me, "I missed you."

The day passes like a dream and ends with Obel, Seb and Connor joining us. Connor simply nods at his son, who smiles briefly and then intently cleans his glasses. It is a stark contrast to the reunion between Obel and his parents. Regrets, memories and apologies are held out and passed around, and by the time the food Seb has brought is bubbling on the stove, the kitchen is filled with laughter. Oscar and I stay close together, our fingers entwined. I don't want our hands to ever break apart but later, when Penny asks me to show her to a place she can change Sky's clothes, I let go of him and take her and her tiny baby to my room.

Penny unwraps the blanket from Sky's sweet, small body and lays it on my bed. Placing Sky gently on top of it, Penny sings to her as she eases off her little knitted socks. I stand a way back, half enchanted by those tiny toes and the small snuffles she makes, and half scared, wondering who taught Penny how to be a mother, how she knew how to love a stranger so fully and tenderly. I am about to ask whether she needs water to clean Sky with when Penny, kneeling at the bedside, tickling Sky's feet, looks up to me.

"Nobody knows, Leora," she says with a small, exhilarated smile. "Only me and Blake." Untying the knot that holds Sky's wrapped cotton suit closed, Penny touches Sky's nose with a tiny kiss. She moves the clothing apart and sighs, looking up at me with awed, eager eyes. I take a step nearer but have to stop. Something bubbles at my throat – tears or laughter, I don't know which – but all around us is the perfume of joy: daisies and spring water and toast and Seb's best biscuits. There on Sky's beautiful, perfect tummy, which rises and falls at such a tremendously alive rate, right there I see two sisters, hands clasped, faces close enough to kiss.

The stories aren't pointless. History is not repeating. The sisters are, again, writing their message and promising that all things can be new.

"I knew you would understand," whispers Penny when I fall on my knees and weep and giggle at this small miracle, who lies on a blanket on my bed.

Chapter Forty-four

The box

Oh! A box.

Now, we know that a box is always rather magical – like a hiding place for a secret.

I like boxes, I just don't know how to feel about their lids.

Don't laugh at me – I'm telling you, the lid of a box is worse than any trap humankind have created to snare beasts. But then, the lid is also more wonderful than any closed mouth before a song.

Give me a box and I won't thank you – not right away – not until I know what the lid is there for. The lid of the box has such an allure – who can resist undoing the clasp, or releasing an edge or placing a key in the lock? The lid invites you, it hypnotizes you. It makes you forget.

The lid is meant to keep things separate – to keep you from getting to the thing within, or to keep the thing within from getting to you. You will only know which when the lid is opened, and by then, it will be too late.

You know about the girl who had a box that was locked? She was tantalized by that lid so that it drove her to distraction. Little did she know that the lid was a shield, and when she opened it up all the evil in the world was let out, and it stung her face, bit her lips, slapped her cheeks and pricked her eyes. Oh, what the earth would be if she had never lifted that lid.

And you remember the brothers who allowed the box to be opened because of their greed? That lid had kept their own hearts safe, for truly, although the gifts were good, the men were not, and they made the gifts become millstones around their necks.

I know of another box. A box with a lid that should not be lifted, not because the content will harm or hinder but because humankind cannot be trusted to care for what is within.

But what is a box if the lid is never lifted?

It is a coffin, of course.

What is this box you hold in your hands? Dare you open it? Are you brave enough, are you good enough and stout of heart? If you have any hesitation I beg of you to bury that box in the ground, for we cannot bear another day of evil.

The story comes to me when I draw, as though Mel herself is next to me. I look around in wonder and shake my head at my tired mind's tricks. My picture is of a box – a precious box that is beginning to crack open.

Chapter Forty-five

When I dream again that night, I dream in screams.

I am running through the forest, vines and briars clutching at my ankles, the heavy sound of pursuit driving me on and on. Ahead, in the distance, are the screams and shrieks of people in agony. I'm too late; I will not get there. Hope is dashed, but still I run. I run until I reach a vast river, a river too fast and wild to cross. Those chasing me are hot on my heels and those who need me are crying out in vain. I stop and almost dive in – rather that than listen to my failure.

All of a sudden two women are with me, one at my left, one at my right. One has skin like mine, full of ink, and the other's is empty. Both have ferocious determination in their eyes.

"You're ready, aren't you, little light?" they demand. And they take my hands, draw me back and then, with all the power of the wind and waves and fire and thunder, they swing me, they hurl me, and I fly.

I am putting on my boots before I have even fully woken up. I have to go – the where and why will have to wait. I must trust this calling that commands me to go.

Foot follows foot and I run. I get closer to the town and realize the air is different: there is no smoke rising from the hall of judgement; the fire is out. I run harder.

They have tied up Saint, those men and women I once knew as Sana's friends. They have bound the statue of Saint as though he were a dangerous beast. With fierce yells they haul on the ropes until the foundations of the statue start to crumble, and with shouts of triumph they heave again. Our Saint comes crashing down, head smashed in to the stone slabs of the town square. Hollers come from the hall of judgement as the vandals laugh and caw at the dousing of the flames. Hurtling past me into the square come men and women of Saintstone, ready to defend, willing to fight.

I hold back; I cannot tell why. I wait and close my eyes, trying to return to my dream, straining to feel their fingers at my wrists: "Moriah and Belia," I whisper, "where will you send me?" And then my eye is drawn to an open door – the fire escape. The museum: someone is in the museum. The sisters' hands bid me go and I run in the dark towards the open door.

There is no mob, no sound of smashing or destruction. I walk silently through the room of curios and creeping horror and peer into the grand foyer. Piled against the locked main doors are bales of straw and the stink of them tells me enough – they have been doused in fuel, ready to burn. I can hear the voices more clearly now and I creep up the stone steps, hoping that their curve will hide me. All of a sudden, they are in view. Sana and Jack. Sana has an oil lantern at her feet and in its flickering light their shadows are all angles and edges, lending a theatrical tone to their bitter words.

"We've always wanted the same thing, haven't we, Jack? I could see it in you even when you were a child. This isn't about taking sides or fighting for our people – we fight for ourselves and no one else."

Minnow shines in the lamplight – like a mockery of Saint, he stands tall.

"You loved your people once, Sana. The embers still glow faintly – how can I be sure your love won't flicker to flame once again? This is your weakness, for you need their love too. Oh, you mistreat them, and you flog them into obedience, but you have them in awe of you. You could not bear it if they all hated you. For you, power over them is not enough – you need their love. That was Dan Longsight's mistake. It's one I won't make."

"You're no better than me, Jack. Let's work together – a fire would serve us both. I would be the undisputed saviour of Featherstone and you would have your people's anger – their rage. You could lead them in any direction then."

"Saviour of Featherstone? Listen to yourself, Sana. There is no Featherstone, you have nothing to save – this is a fight you can't win. You need land and wealth. Setting our museum on fire, knocking down our statue, putting out the fire of judgement – it only wins you Saintstone's ire. They won't back down. You will never get all that you want."

"Fight me then, Jack. It's what you've wanted all this time, so come on." Minnow glares, his hands poised as though ready to grasp her neck. He holds himself back, but only just. "Aren't you going to stop me, Jack? Just think, all these books – this is where you've stored them, right? All I have to do is drop this lantern on those bales and your precious museum is history. You can't just watch those skin books burn – I know you too well." She pushes her hair out of her face and grins, eyes glittering. She shifts her stance, readying for the attack that will surely come.

But then, that laugh. The same laugh I heard when he showed me Gull. A laugh that gloats in victory already won.

"Why would I stop you?" Minnow breathes. "What kind of fool do you think I am? Your little tantrums are my very greatest political strength. Haven't you noticed, Sana? Every time you hurt this town, the people's love for me gets stronger. Every victory you celebrate has been planned by me. You only succeed when I allow you to: your miserable attempt to kill Longsight is ample proof. There is always only one winner in these fights: you get weaker and I get more glorious. Just imagine how they would praise the leader who raged against this latest attack. If I can be seen to weep over the loss of some skin books, these dull people will adore me." He takes a step closer. "Oh, it's fun to have an enemy – even one as pitiful as you, because it lets the people think they are in danger. And scared people are the easiest to beguile – it is so simple to exploit them. But of course, you know that." Jack Minnow smiles at Sana. "Burn this whole place down, Sana. It will be the best thing that's ever happened to me."

She pauses, looks about her as though hoping for support, and as she glances round I know she sees me. A small smile rises on her face and she bends down, picks up the lantern and acts as if cowed, she is ready to leave. At the last moment she lifts the burning lantern and swings it, smashing it into Jack Minnow's shocked face. He falls to the ground, hitting his head hard. Glass breaks and the lantern almost goes out. Sana hurtles past me, she makes one quick swipe at the bales with the shattered lantern and I hear the *whoomph* of fresh fire. I can't let her go.

I skid into the room of the blanks just in time to see Sana stop and plant the lantern on the glass tank. She grins as she places both hands on the edge of the tank and starts to push. Her face, ghoulish in the lantern light, stretches in horrible glee, and I realize what she is trying to do. I rush forward and brace myself against the other side. I can't let her win.

But Sana is strong, and her eyes are wild. She changes her grip to the bottom edge of the glass tank – I can see the liquid inside moving, hear the unearthly groan and creak of skin against wet glass as the man sways. And she heaves – her legs, her back, her arms, her desperation all too powerful for me to hold back. The tank breaks free from its base and I shout out, "Sana, no – the lantern!"

But this was her plan all along.

The tank – the box – hits the ground edge first and the *crack* sounds like stone on skull. Time slows and each shatter and fracture that spreads across the glass grows like a frost, until, all of a sudden, comes the flood.

The man's body hits the floor with a sickening thud and the fluid gushes like a tsunami across the floor towards me, pushing Sana towards the open door and forcing me back, deeper into the museum. The smell is chemical, and when the lantern falls the flame does not need to touch liquid – the fumes are enough. With an explosive punch, a ball of fire is launched.

Chapter Forty-six

I run towards the atrium. I need to save the books. I know all too well that there is no way out of this place – not at night. The fire is already roaring and pluming smoke. My eyes burn, and my throat tightens, and I know I have reached my final chapter. There is no rescue, there is no saviour; there is just me and fire and smoke. But there is one final thing I can do. I cover my face with my shawl and race up the stone steps, which are a mist of smoke. I almost trip but I dip my head and press on. I run on past the stories and the precious place Dad would always bring me. The smoke is too thick up here and I can't get my bearings. I pause and look about me – a mistake.

Jack Minnow reaches me, grabs me by my hair and pulls me across to the open central space where the lantern windows above usually pour down sunlight on to all the floors. He holds me against the parapet, and I fight back as he tries to lift me over it to drop me on the stone and flame below. Shards of glass gleam from his face, blood runs into his eyes. He attempts to wipe it away, and as he changes his handhold on me, I pull free. I should run but I can't take my eyes off him as he rises up once again, roaring at me with hatred and pain. I don't mean to do it — I do not plan it — but when I pile into him, to make him stop, to get him away from me, he stumbles backwards, hips clashing into the barrier. It is like watching a monster in fog, and above the shout of the flames, I hear him yell, arms windmilling as he overbalances and fights to right himself. A bluster of smoke chokes me, and I turn to hide my stinging eyes. When the smoke passes, all that is left is the empty space where Minnow stood before he fell.

In my horror, all I can do is run again. But it is so much harder this time — the heat and the smoke are too much. I am lost — at the top of a narrow flight of steps, away from the main museum. I think I'm hallucinating now, just dreaming of a different place because the reality is too awful to bear. And then I hear it — a rhythmic bang at the door that faces me. I know where I am now, and I know who is knocking.

Searing my hand on the key, I turn it, screaming out in pain. The door swings open to reveal a scarecrow woman with matted red hair. The tracks of tears shine pale in her ashen face. I turn, scrambling across the ground now. I must carry on.

Finally, I reach the place I have been aiming for,

crawling along, trying to find the least clogged part of the air. I am here, with the books.

Skin books cower in their boxes and on shelves as though in cages and coops. I lift a metal bookend, which is etched with the letters D–F, and grasp it in both hands, my burned skin screaming. I smash it against the corner of the window, again and again, until there is the beginning of a crack. The heat does the next part and the glass creaks and shatters. I kick against the remaining bars and finally enough space is cleared. My throat begs at me to pant – to get air into my tired lungs, but I resist, holding my hand over my covered mouth. I don't have much time; my body is already tingling, my vision swirling. I reach up and gather books into my arms, hurling them from the window. I think I see them spread their wings and flap, beating against the breeze and smoke, soaring until they come to land. More books fly, and I release book after book into the cool night air. Black wings flutter, ash falls, paper flies.

But I can't free every book; I beg their pages and covers to take off, to drift. But smoke soon wraps its arms around me and grips me with its needy fingers. When it covers my mouth and whispers into my ear, I assent, and with it, I descend.

Chapter Forty-seven

The girl.

There was a girl.

Just a girl.

She loved stories, because in the stories her father told her, there was always a girl and she always got rescued. A knight would slay a dragon. A prince would rouse a princess with a kiss. A handsome man would climb a rope of hair. And the girl? She would learn, she would understand, and she would be safe – kept by her rescuer, happily ever after.

And so the girl grew up unafraid, because she knew that although she may face dragons, curses and tall towers, there would always be a rescue.

When her father passed away, she felt all the more like a girl in one of the stories – for in them, the parents always died and then the catastrophes would begin.

She waited for a dragon, but one never came. Instead there was a different beast that threw fire at her.

She looked out, watchful for a curse that would make her sleep.

And yet the things she saw terrified her so completely she felt she would never sleep again.

She longed for her tower. But instead she was buried under misery and treachery. Her hair was cut before it ever grew long enough to be a rope.

When she found herself in a deep and melancholy pit, she cried out, sure that her prince would be riding by soon, ready to come to her aid. Her back ached and her nails split, and her clothes were torn to rags.

Again, she called out, but it only attracted predators and they circled the edge of the pit, biding their time. Surely, she thought, surely this is the time for my rescuer to come? And she shouted again until her voice was lost. This time her call brought a rain cloud and the pit began to fill with water.

There she was: in a hole too deep, with beasts licking their lips at its edge and the waters rising. She waited.

She waited until the water was up to her ankles and she gazed into the sky ready to welcome her rescuer when he arrived.

She waited until the water was up to her knees, and still he did not come.

She waited until the water was up to her waist and she sighed.

Her only choices were death, or a rescue, and no hero was going to come.

And so, the girl closed her eyes, and while the cloud poured ice-cold water down upon her, she imagined.

She imagined a story where the girl was able to calm the dragon and they were friends.

She imagined a story where the girl set her alarm clock and woke up without any great trouble.

She imagined a story where the high tower was her greatest haven, and she kept her hair short.

And, as she imagined, her back began to tickle, and then to itch, and then to burn and then to sear. She opened her eyes and looked around at the slick walls, up at the terrible creatures, and down at the rising flood. But she did not weep; she was no longer afraid. The girl shook her shoulders and two great black wings gave a satisfyingly deep crack. She breathed in and she knew without any doubt that the wings would hold her.

Up she rose, the wings a pulse, a throb of held-back power. Out of the water, out of the pit, past the beasts. Away she flew, beautiful black wings beating powerfully. Knowing more freedom in that one moment than she had felt in all her life.

Girl rescues girl. Girl flies. And when no one is watching, girl soars to the stars.

Chapter Forty-eight

Breathe in.

Breathe out.

Breathe in.

Breathe out.

Keep going.

Never stop.

Breathe in.

Breathe out.

For the rest of your life.

Can you hear me? I have no voice, not since the smoke.

Breathe in.

Breathe out.

They say to just keep breathing — all I have to do is stay alive.

But that's a lot. Can I just have a rest? Can I take a little break from breathing? It hurts. I'll come back; just let me be quiet and still now.

Can you see me? It takes some getting used to.

Breathe in.

Breathe out.

My body is healing itself, they tell me. But I don't know.

They took skin from my legs and back and stomach to fix my arms and hands. I am a patchwork of pieces. A puzzle unmade.

Can you touch me? Am I still marked?

Breathe in.

Breathe out.

Or are these just scars? Who knows how to put me together again? Who can read my story now? Do you know what it says?

Can you love me? Am I enough?

Breathe in.

Breathe out.

Just a girl. Surrounded by souls that are so beautiful. I can see your soul. You are good.

And I have wings.

Chapter Forty-nine

One year later

I am woken by a kiss on the back of my hand. His is the first face I see and, although it hurts a little, I can't help but smile.

"I didn't mean to disturb you," Oscar whispers. "Your mum said it would be OK to come and say hi."

Oscar was there every day I spent in the hospital and we've been together every day since. He tells me that he and Fenn have grand plans to go back to Featherstone one day and start using the bricks that were left from the wall. They want to build a pathway through the forest, joining our towns. But there's time for that. For now, we are adjusting to how everything has changed.

We've been waiting for the next attack. There has been no sign of Sana or her gang, and some say they're gone for good. But I know they're out there, somewhere. We have learned not to be so foolish – we are not the strongest or the greatest. We are just us.

And *us* is a strange bunch.

Jack Minnow's body was never found, and although there were rumours for a while that he was seen running from the burning town, those have died down. I still wake from dreams where I see his face before he fell. With Minnow gone, we needed a new leader. Someone chosen by the people.

There are signs that we might have something like a government again soon. It turned out that Mel was the one who put her arms around me and leapt out of the museum's window. She could see people below holding a blanket calling at us to jump. She had spent months in the room with the books of the storytellers, locked away, being kept alive by Minnow, who knows why. But once she recovered, the vote was clear – Mel is in charge of things here in Saintstone.

Oscar climbs under the covers with me and we lie nose to nose whispering about our plans for the day. He runs his fingers up my arm.

"Did you feel that?" he asks when I shiver. Biting my lip, I nod – my nerve damage is improving all the time. His hand moves higher and I quiver again. The warmth of his body makes my cheeks flush and I press closer. His brown eyes close and I plant kisses across his jaw. His sigh switches something in me and I am greedy for his skin, his chest, his mouth. There is no space between us. Finally, I am home.

There has been so much to change, so much to disagree on. How do you bring blanks and marked together after all these years? After all this hatred? I think we're still trying to work that out. Tanya and Solomon live nearby now, on the outskirts of Saintstone. It's not easy, but they told Mum that nowhere felt quite like home any more. At least this way they can be close to Obel and Gull. Fenn flits from place to place, always on the lookout for a new challenge and thrill. The Whitworths have been kind, gracious and wise. The people of Saintstone are slowly warming to them and accepting them as the good people they are. Julia went to Tanya for advice last week – I think she's worried about Seb's growing desire for independence – and Tanya's joy at being asked was beautiful. I'm learning something about patience from them.

I'm glad Seb is pestering his parents about being more independent. He proved himself to be clear-thinking and careful when he took care of Mum – and his kindness. . . well, if I can become more like him I will be proud. He was the bravest of us all when he had nothing to gain from it.

Living with Mum is calmer than I expected it to be. Her motto of "keep your head down" is long gone, and

I feel like I'm seeing the true her for the first time. She is still a reader, in the fullest sense of the word. People come to her for counsel now – her insights, whether they come from people's ink or their words, are life-giving and full of peace. She blooms.

Gull is . . . Gull. She seems at home with herself for the first time. We spend time together playing card games – it's been the safest way for us to rebuild the bridges between us. I think we both try to let the other win. I made her laugh yesterday – that helpless gulping giggle – and I thought it sounded like hope. When the three of us spent the evening together recently, Verity asked Gull what she believed. I was afraid that the question would trigger terrible memories, but Gull was thoughtful and she told us that she didn't know and that she was happy that way. She has fought for faith and I've seen her so broken as she has been trying to recover. She is healthy today, and for now, that is because she is staying clear of landing herself on any one thing. She makes me smile every day.

Karl and Obel work together in the studio. Some days they fight but I think they're more like brothers than colleagues. Obel has had his hand reset and is dutiful in his therapy. Both his recovery and the business are going well. Karl comes and tells me the news; I like it.

Obel once told me that there was always redemption. It sounded so noble when he said it and it gave me hope.

But my resolve has been tested over this last year – do I really believe in second, third, fourth chances?

He apologized for marking me that morning in the hall of judgment. When he reopened the studio, he asked me to pay a visit. It took a lot out of me, but, with Verity's help, I made it. He had the chair ready and, confusingly, clippers set up too. Verity smiled and I knew she was in on whatever plans Obel had been making.

"You know, Leora – it's not done to double up with ink." He smiled. "I've already done one crow tattoo on you – two is just greedy. Besides, it's not quite right for you – not your style." My hair is still short from being burned away and I didn't mind him shaving the back of my head again.

I am much better with pain these days – I barely registered the needle as he worked and Verity distracted me by speaking animatedly about a boy she likes. I was glad when Obel was finished though, eager to see what he'd done. I looked in the mirror and he held up another, so I could see what the mark was. Verity gasped. I could still see parts of the crow – blackened claws and feathers, but this was no crow, not any more. From the charred remains Obel made grow plumes of orange, red and teal. A phoenix stands guard behind me now.

"When you rise from the ashes, nothing can keep you down. You, girl, you're on fire."

I am glad to be alive; at least, I am now. I love my new skin, which has been stretched to fit me. There are glimpses of the old me between the cracks and I sometimes smile when I notice some ink I've not spotted before. The mark of the sisters is gone, and I miss them, but I am getting used to being the patchwork girl. Some people say I am an emblem: a picture of the future, of marks that exist and don't exist all at once. I am tired of being anything but Leora, though, and I tell them so. I have regular appointments to help me get movement and sensation and flexibility back – I will be an inker again. I will.

I met a child in the hospital waiting room yesterday and she asked me whether I was sad about all my scars.

I looked at my arms and saw the puckered edges, the shine of burned skin, the zig-zag mending of grafted skin. I am all scar tissue.

I told the girl that I loved my scars. And I do. My scars tell my story more clearly than any ink. I was broken and now I am whole. But the cracks still show – lightning flashes that say, "You can't keep me down."

Because there's redemption. There is always redemption.

And with redemption comes the freedom to fly.

Acknowledgements

Thank you, Jo Unwin and all at JULA.

Thank you to the brilliant team at Scholastic for making this book happen:

Gen Herr, Lauren Fortune, Andrew Biscomb, Jamie Gregory, Harriet Dunlea, Tanya Harris-Brown, Emily Landy, Pete Matthews, Jessica White, Emma Jobling and Olivia Horrox.

Scholastic has been a wonderful home for this trilogy, and I have been nurtured with such kindness and expertise. Thank you for making my publishing journey so special; I couldn't have wished for a better place to belong.

Thank you to friends and family for your love, patience and support. I am lucky to have you in my life. Heartfelt thanks to the nurses of Ward 8 at Royal Preston Hospital, where I wrote some of this book, marvelling at how you cared for my kid. Long live the NHS.

Thanks to Jenny Salisbury and Sheila Irvine who each shared their expertise with me. Thanks to Dave Winn at Market Quarter Tattoo: I finally know what it feels like.

Mikey, Dan and Jemima: books are nice, but you three are my true treasures. Your stories are going to be so, so beautiful.

ALICE BROADWAY

Alice's first book, *Ink*, was one of the bestselling YA debuts of 2017 and was shortlisted for many prizes, including the Books Are My Bag YA category and the Waterstones Children's Book Prize Older Fiction category.

Alice drinks more tea than is really necessary and loves writing in her yellow camper van.